THE KAZILLION WISH

NICK PLACE

Illustrated by
ROSS COLLINS

The Chicken House

SCHOLASTIC INC.
NEW YORK

To Lightning Rod, the One Who Moves the Stars,
and the woman who gave me both

Text copyright © 2003 by Nick Place
Illustrations copyright © 2004 by Ross Collins

First published by Allen and Unwin, Sydney, Australia

First published in the United Kingdom in 2005 by The Chicken House,
2 Palmer Street, Frome, Somerset BA11 1DS.
www.doublecluck.com

Library of Congress Cataloging-in-Publication Data available

ISBN 0-439-69215-6

10 9 8 7 6 5 4 3 2 1   05 06 07 08 09

Printed in the U.S.A.   23
First American edition, April 2005

The display type was set in EatwellChubby.
The text type was set in 12-pt. Garamond.
Book design by Ian Butterworth and Leyah Jensen

CONTENTS

1

Things Aren't Good

Harlan and Ainsley Banana were having a bad day. Actually, the entire week hadn't been great. Come to think of it, they'd been in the soup for a few months. In fact, if you really sat down and thought it through, it was three years since they had been genuinely happy.

Three years ago, Harlan and Ainsley's parents decided not to live together and their dad moved into a house a couple of streets away. Harlan had been eight years old when it happened, and Ainsley had only been four. When you're four, you don't even know why the air is see-through or why water is wet, let alone why your parents would suddenly start living in two different houses, but that didn't stop it from happening.

Harlan and Ainsley were now old enough to understand that their parents had separated for good. They knew this wasn't a fight over a toy or the last piece of cake, and that this couldn't be solved with a group hug. Harlan was the deep thinker of the kids, but he had been strangely quiet about the new living arrangements, so it was left to Ainsley to ask questions like "Why aren't you and Dad together anymore?" or "When are you and Mom going to move back into the same house?" or even "Now that you're not married, am I still your daughter?" That last one got an unexpected laugh out of their dad, who usually just looked sad whenever she tried to make some sense of it all.

Not that everything was bad about having two houses. Their parents didn't scream at each other anymore. In fact, they seemed to get along pretty well, in a strange, polite sort of way. When the kids were passed from one parent to the other, they'd even exchange a few words, ask about each other's health and things like that. Harlan was becoming wise to how people reacted, and he was pleased that his parents no longer drove each other crazy.

There were other good things, too: double the toys and double the pets. It didn't come close to making up for their parents' split, but when Dad moved into his new house, he produced a whole bunch of new toys to help Harlan and Ainsley settle in. Harlan got a *Star Wars* bedspread, and Ainsley finally moved on from Teletubbies and slept between *Dexter's Laboratory* sheets. Ainsley also had lots of pencils, crayons, and other drawing stuff at both houses, while Harlan had Harry Potter toys at his mom's place and superhero figurines at his dad's. That part was cool.

The pets were cooler. Dad bought a kitten, a

chocolate brown Burmese called Scramble — Dad said he was named after the state of his brain. Scramble was awesome. He had the most amazingly silky fur, which he licked clean for hours at a time. He had spectacularly green eyes and his fur was a darker brown around his face, ears, and paws, so that he looked like he was wearing a mask and magnificent boots. When he wasn't washing himself, Scramble often snoozed in the sunshine, but he was happiest when the kids were around. He flew down the hall chasing balls of crumpled-up paper, went crazy if he discovered a cobweb hanging off his ear, and pounced on Ainsley's bare feet as she walked quietly to the bathroom early in the morning.

At night, Scramble would leap onto one of their beds with an intense look on his face, refusing even to blink, and would burrow until he was under the sheet and next to one of the children's bodies, pushing them out of bed for the rest of the night by leaning hard.

"How can a cat so small be so strong?" Ainsley said after waking up yet again to find herself teetering on the edge of the mattress while Scramble the cat was curled up in a tiny, satisfied ball right in the middle of the bed.

"It's as though he puts all four paws against an invisible brick wall and pushes backward," said Harlan.

"An invisible brick wall?"

"Maybe I dreamed that," Harlan admitted.

"You always have better dreams than me. I was dreaming about a math test."

"Tragic!" said Harlan, watching his sister trying to move the cat and getting a gentle nip on the finger in response. "If that were me, I'd toss Scramble out of bed so I could sleep."

"Well, I'm not you and I like it," Ainsley replied. She pulled the bedspread back over her and Scramble, snuggled into his warm, furry body, then tickled his ear until he purred.

Mom went one better than a cat. She got a boyfriend named Philip. He was an accountant, although he made a big deal of the fact that he was in a rock band a long time ago. He was forever playing cassette tapes of old bands the kids had never heard of, featuring a lot of thrashing guitars. Harlan would roll his eyes, go to his room, and put on his own CDs, featuring excellent new bands with a lot of thrashing guitars. Philip was OK, though. Mom was happier now that he was around.

Mom had also bought a guinea pig, which was good to cuddle but didn't actually do much. Ainsley named it Log. The only time Log ever showed any sign of action was when Ainsley let him out of his cage and he took off around the yard. One time, Harlan stood back thinking there must be a way to trap Log in a corner of the yard. Meanwhile, Ainsley ran full speed at the small hedge Log was hiding under, to try to scare him out. Mom finally pounced on him near the back shed. She got sticks and leaves in her hair, and her clothes were dirty and sopping — the result of the grass just being watered. Harlan laughed as his disheveled mother trooped back to the guinea pig cage with the tiny escapee. She said Log should have been called Houdini after a famous escape artist from years ago. Ainsley gave Log some extra lettuce to help him overcome the trauma of the chase.

So life had changed a lot over the past three years, and Harlan and Ainsley had learned to adapt. They were now used to carting clothes, pajamas, and homework between the two houses a couple of times a week, and were resigned to having to tell the same stories twice, first to one parent and then to the other.

Actually, Ainsley liked telling the same stories twice because they got better the more times she told them. Her performance on Sports Day was impressive when she told Mom about it Tuesday night, but by Friday, when she told Dad, she had practically beaten Olympic records!

They now expected their parents to sit separately at school concerts, even if that stank. (It was hard enough to spot one parent in the crowd to make sure they were watching your every move, let alone two.) The worst days were birthdays. Both Harlan and Ainsley still felt a twinge whenever their birthday parties had only Mom or Dad in charge of the cake. Never both. Not good.

But that didn't mean life couldn't get worse. A few months earlier, the school year had started badly when both Banana kids found they had rotten teachers at Fruitfly Bay Elementary School. Harlan was in fifth grade. His teacher was a man named Alfred Stranglenose, who looked about one hundred twenty years old, was cloud-threateningly tall, and had a habit of finishing every question with "yes?" which freaked out all the students.

On day two of the school year, Harlan knew he was in trouble.

"Harlan Banana, what is the capital of France, yes?" Stranglenose asked, his head somewhere near the clouds.

Harlan had no idea if he was supposed to say "Paris"

or "no" or "yes" or "Paris, yes?" Or was there another country he hadn't even heard of called "Franceyes"? No, that would be pronounced "Frank Eyes," which wasn't a bit like France.

"Um, Paris," Harlan eventually mumbled.

"Very good, Banana. That's right, yes?"

Harlan sat there, blinking. Was he supposed to answer the yes or shut up? He didn't even know if the correct answer was "Paris" or "Umparis." Maybe somewhere there was a country called Frank Eyes where the capital city was Umparis.

Harlan's classes were a nightmare.

Ainsley, down in second grade, was faring even worse. Two words: Ms. Grassmuncher. (The naughty kids at the back of the classroom had already dubbed her "The Lawnmower.")

Ms. Grassmuncher spoke so slowly that half the students nodded off in every single class. "OK . . . (pause) . . . class . . . (pause) . . . today . . . (double pause) . . . . . . we will . . . be . . . studying . . . math . . . times . . . tables . . . . so . . . turn . . . to . . . page . . . twenty . . . (everybody had time here to turn to page twenty) . . . six . . . (hurried flipping of six more pages) . . . and . . . let's . . . (incredibly long pause here) . . . . begin with . . . the fives . . . times . . . table."

It was unbearable. Even worse, when a kid blatantly fell asleep, Ms. Grassmuncher's response was truly evil. Like the time James Windscreen went nose-first — *bang!* — onto his desktop, or Talia Antfinder started snoring really loudly. Ainsley watched in horror as Talia snored, oblivious to The Lawnmower's nasty sneer. Ms. Grassmuncher grabbed a wooden ruler from near the blackboard. "Talia," Ainsley hissed. "Talia, wake up!" But it was too late. The ruler slammed down in front of Talia with a wood-splintering crash. She woke with such a jump that her knees smashed into the base of her desk. Some of the other kids thought the whole episode was hilarious, but Ainsley didn't. Ainsley always ran around so much at lunchtime that she found it almost impossible to stay awake when Grassmuncher was in slow motion and the afternoon sun was warm through the glass. This meant she was a likely victim for slamming timber, major shock, and bruised knees, just like poor Talia.

So, that was the last few months. But even against this grim backdrop, the past week had been really bad for Harlan and Ainsley, and it had nothing to do with teachers. It had to do with their father. His name was Spencer, but Harlan and Ainsley called him Dad. On a good day, he called Harlan "Snarlin' Harlan" and Ainsley "Second Banana." On a good day, the second day of the weekend would be officially declared "Banana Sunday," and Dad would take them both for fantastic ice-cream sundaes and chocolate milk shakes at the local café. On a good day, Spencer Banana took the kids fishing, surfing, swimming, Frisbee-throwing, or a combination of all those things. But there hadn't been many good days lately.

On a bad day, Dad would get the mopes. He'd pick them up (the kids, not the mopes) from school as usual on a Dad Day, but he'd be kind of quiet. Harlan would look at Ainsley, and Ainsley would glance at Harlan. Usually, Dad had pop music playing and would sing loudly while driving, but on a bad day the music would be sad and there'd be no singing. No singing at all. Ainsley would start telling him about how the water from the water fountain went up her nose, but then she would realize he was just saying "Uh-huh" and she knew he wasn't really listening. Harlan would try to show him the space project he was working on, but Dad would nod absently instead of digging out a book on the moon landing. For dinner, he'd halfheartedly cook sausages and potatoes, which were tasty enough but not very inspired for the dad who could turn dinnertime into a pirate night, complete with fish and chips and eye patches and no food served unless you added an "Ahoy, me hearty!" to your request for a Pirate Pink Milk (strawberry milk) or more Cutlassed Spuds (French fries).

This past week, Dad had world-record mopes. A couple of nights ago, Harlan and Ainsley lay in bed and heard him on the phone to his friend Tony. Dad was whispering that he was lonely, which they couldn't understand because they were there, and what were they — chopped liver?

"Dad?" Ainsley asked in the morning, halfway through breakfast. "Why do you get lonely if we're here?"

"What?"

"I heard you on the phone last night. You said that you were lonely, but we're here. We're here a lot. How come you get lonely when Harlan and I are around so much?"

Dad looked at them for a long time, so long that Ainsley thought that even Ms. Grassmuncher would struggle to come up with such a pause.

"There are different kinds of lonely, Second Banana. I hope you never have to understand that."

Later, on the way to school, Harlan and Ainsley were lost in thought.

"Do you have any idea what Dad meant?" Ainsley asked.

"I'm not sure. I think it's an adult thing he's going through. I think that's what he meant," said Harlan.

"He was playing 'the music' again last night."

"I know. The sad songs."

The next day was today. Remember how, at the very start, I mentioned that Harlan and Ainsley Banana were having a bad day, on top of a bad week, bad last few months, and bad past three years? Well, we're finally through all those bad times and up to today, which was — just to make sure there's no misunderstanding — a particularly bad day.

It began with Ainsley drowning. Well, actually, she wasn't drowning, she was dreaming, but she thought she was drowning until she realized that she had wet the bed, which hardly ever happened, now that she was seven. Sometimes, when she was in a really deep sleep, she'd dream of rock pools and waves crashing and waterfalls and garden hoses, and all of a sudden she'd realize that she needed to go to the bathroom — *really badly* — but by then it was too late and she had wet her bed. Dad was still half asleep as he changed her sheets, but he mumbled something understanding before he stumbled back to his own bed. Not a great start to the day for Ainsley.

Harlan discovered that, during the night, a mosquito had bitten him right on the end of his nose, so it was all swollen, like a clown's. When he touched it, he cried out, and when he rubbed in some anti-itch cream, it hurt even more. He looked like a complete joke. Not a great start to the day for Harlan, either.

Breakfast was worse. Dad hadn't reappeared from bed after helping Ainsley change her sheets a couple of hours earlier. A dig in the fridge revealed that Dad had no milk, so cereal was out of the picture. Plus, there was only enough bread for one piece of toast each. Harlan smothered his with jam, but the single slice only made him feel hungry for more food. Dad really needed to do some shopping.

In the end, Harlan sat morosely munching on dry crackers covered with butter and cheese, which was actually not too bad, but well short of his hopes of Coco Pops or other sugary delights. On a good Dad Day, Spencer Banana would have been up before either of them, would have had music booming through the house, and would have been elbow-deep in breakfast preparation — bacon and eggs, or even pancakes, to set them up for a day of action and adventure. He would have made plans, and Harlan would have been dying to find out what they were.

But today, Dad's bedroom door was closed and his room dark. It was up to Harlan to think of a plan. As he reached for another cracker, he noticed a pile of old LP records — like they used to play back in the old days — on the chair next to the table. A couple of them had the letters DD written on them in marker and one also had an X and a heart shape. There was a notepad as well, and in Dad's handwriting were the words: "DD now?"

Harlan munched on the dry crackers and cheese. What was that all about?

2

Make a Wish

Dad finally staggered out of bed mid-morning and immediately made them turn off the television and go outside. So much for being glad to see him. Harlan's bike had a flat tire, so riding was out. Ainsley's sandal strap broke and there'd been lots of bees around this summer so she was forced to put on sneakers, even though it was going to be 90 degrees, which meant "hot."

So, the day was going badly. Really badly. Harlan found Ainsley lying on the front lawn, scratching Scramble behind the ears while the cat washed his fur. They sat in the sun in silence for a while.

"Ainsley, if you had one wish, what would it be?" Harlan asked.

Hmmm. Ainsley had a big think, smiling as Scramble's rough, ticklish tongue moved from his fur to her finger. Eventually, she said, "To be able to talk to cats. What about you?"

Harlan took even longer before he finally came up with an answer. "I think my wish would be to ride a dolphin."

Ainsley laughed. "That would definitely be cool!"

"Yeah, dream on, right? C'mon, let's see what Dad's doing. He must have cheered up by now."

They wandered back inside where their dad was sitting at the kitchen table, still nursing his first coffee of the day and listlessly flicking through the sports section of the newspaper.

"Hey, Dad, let's go to the park." Ainsley was full of energy.

Spencer Banana looked at them vaguely. "It's pretty early, isn't it?"

"It's almost eleven," Harlan said.

"Really? Oh. Sorry. I hardly got any sleep last night. I had one of those nights where I kept trying to sleep, but my brain just wouldn't stop running around inside my head."

"Your brain runs around? Like with legs?"

"I don't think Dad meant it that literally, Ainsley. This sleeping thing is a bit of a problem, Dad."

"I know, Harlan. Trust me, I don't want to be awake. I had all these big plans for today. It was going to be a spectacular Dad Day, one of the best Dad Days in history. I was thinking soccer, surfing, maybe even try to get a kite into the air."

"Well, it's only eleven o'clock. We can still do lots of stuff."

"Yeah, I guess. I'm just so tired. How about I finish

the newspaper and my coffee and then maybe see how we're doing?"

Ainsley was still in action mode. "Well, how about me and Harlan go down to the beach and check out the surf?"

"'Harlan and I,' not 'me and Harlan.'"

"You want to go with Harlan? I said I'd go with Harlan."

"No, I mean you should have said . . . oh, never mind. It's a great idea. You two go to the beach, and I'll try to get my act together."

So now Harlan and Ainsley were headed toward Fruitfly Bay itself, across the park between the shopping center and the beach. They were both pretty quiet.

"Dad's just so mopey. We've got to do something," said Ainsley.

"That's for sure," said Harlan. "I'm not certain about this because I'm not an adult, but I think I know what's wrong."

"You do?" Ainsley adored her big brother. She wouldn't go so far as to say he was smarter than she was, but he did think a lot and he did know a few things she didn't.

"I might have an even better wish than riding a dolphin. I think what Dad needs is somebody to love, like he used to love Mom." Harlan said this very carefully and glanced at his little sister to see if this might upset her, but she was frowning and her bottom lip was caught under her teeth, which was a sign that she was concentrating hard.

"A new mom?" she said.

"No, not a new mom. Mom is Mom. But a new someone for Dad. Somebody who'll still be there when we're not around. We know he's not lonely for kids, at least not on Dad Days, and he said it was a different kind of loneliness. I figure he needs a new wife."

Ainsley looked at her brother with giant eyes. "But not a new mom, Harlan?"

"No, Ainsley. That would be completely different. If Dad got a new wife, it would mean we'd have Mom, who will always be Mom, *and* an also-mom, living with Dad, who might love us, too."

"An also-mom?" Ainsley was biting her lip again. "An also-mom could make sure there's enough milk and bread for breakfast."

"An also-mom would know what to do when Dad starts to play that sad music, like last night."

"And she would remember to dry our swimsuits between swimming lessons so we don't have to wear wet and smelly suits a week later."

"Dad only did that twice, Ainsley."

"Even so, I like the idea of an also-mom! Let's get one. Is there a shop?"

"No, no shops." Harlan got a lot of laughs out of his sister sometimes.

The main question for Harlan wasn't *how* to find an also-mom, rather it was *should* they find an also-mom. The vibe kids get from adults is that they should stay out of "adult matters," but Harlan had never really understood why. What was wrong with trying to help out Dad when he was miserable? Just because something seemed to be out of his control didn't mean he shouldn't use his imagination to think of possible solutions.

"I have no idea how we would find an also-mom," he said. "I'll have to have a think about it."

"Maybe we should talk to Dad." Ainsley was skipping now, unable to simply walk when she was in action mode.

"Not today, the way he's moping. I'm staying clear of him."

Suddenly, Ainsley's eyes grew wide and she took off across the grass, running as fast as she could. "I've got it, Harlan! Come on!"

"What?" Harlan ran after her but even though she was so much younger, Ainsley was fast. After 50 yards he was slowly catching up but still had no idea where they were running. Ainsley was chasing something and, whatever it was, it was moving, because her head jerked from side to side as she kept her eyes on it. Then she slowed down, holding her hands out in front of her. She lunged, looked in her hands, and frowned.

But then she swung her head to her left and took off again, hands out in front as before. This time, she was careful, judging and judging and waiting for the right moment and then lunging again, closing her hands together and stopping dead in her tracks to peep inside her fingers.

At last Harlan was beside her, panting hard. "What is it, Ainsley? What's going on?"

Her eyes were shining. "I've got it. Everything's OK. We can have an also-mom for Dad by lunchtime."

Harlan stared at her. "What on earth have you got in your hands, Ainsley?"

Ainsley opened them just wide enough for her brother to see the fluffy white seedpod of a dandelion resting in there.

"It's a fairy, Harlan. Look, it's even got a wishpod. We can wish for an also-mom."

Harlan sighed. For a moment he had been genuinely excited, thinking Ainsley had a real plan. He should have known better. She was only seven.

"Ainsley, there's no such thing as fairies. That's just a seedpod from a dandelion plant. We're going to need more than that to track down an also-mom."

Ainsley completely ignored him. She looked around to check that nobody was near, walked behind a tree to make sure she had some privacy, and put her lips very gently to her hands. She whispered, "O magical one, I have a wish. Please hear it."

And then there was a slight *pffff* sound, and a burst of light shot out of Ainsley's clasped hand. Instead of a dandelion, a fairylike creature hovered over her palms. She was brilliantly gold and about as tall as a soft-drink can. Her wings were fluttering so fast, the children could barely see them.

Harlan gasped and Ainsley smiled.

The flying creature said,

3

Terms and Conditions

Harlan spoke first. "You're not real!"

The little flying person said, "Well, that's disappointing. For me, anyway."

"Of course she's real, Harlan," said Ainsley. "She's a fairy. I made a wish and here she is!"

"Actually, I'm not a fairy," said the creature. "I'm a frongle."

"Of course you're a fairy," said Ainsley. "I made a wish on a dandelion, and you appeared. That makes you a fairy."

"Well, actually, it doesn't. You know, it's *so* annoying. Somebody starts a rumor, maybe two hundred human years ago, that fairies offer dandelion wishes and boom, frongles — the real hard workers — get left in the fairy dust."

"Are frongles like fairies?" Ainsley soldiered on.

The frongle sighed. "No, not even a bit alike. I am definitely *not* a fairy. You got that? NOT a fairy. You have no idea how sick I am of being called a fairy. Just because we answer dandelion wishes, people assume we're fairies. Floating around at the edge of the yard. La-de-da! Oooh, look at the pretty fairies. Please!"

Harlan and Ainsley stared, unsure what to say to that outburst.

"Right, *not* a fairy," Harlan finally said.

"Got it. A frongle — definitely a frongle," his sister added. "My name is Ainsley and this is my big brother, Harlan."

"Nice to meet you. My name's Zootfrog, from the Fruitfly Bay Frongle Collective."

"Never heard of it," said Harlan.

"Hmm, maybe you know it as the FBFC?"

"I don't think so." Harlan crossed his arms and gave the frongle a look.

"Boy, we've *so* got to work on our marketing," Zootfrog said, then brightened and smiled at Ainsley. "Anyway, what's your wish, cupcakes?"

"Well, it's a big one," Ainsley said uncertainly.

Zootfrog rolled her eyes. "Not a pony. I'm so sick of dishing out ponies to every second little girl."

"No, not big like a pony. Big, like a hugely important wish."

Zootfrog slowed her wings and leaned forward. "An important wish. I don't get asked for many of those. If it's not a pony, it's the latest Harry Potter merchandise, or maybe some chocolate."

"We don't need chocolate," Harlan said. "We've got problems. Well, our dad has, and we need some help."

"I thought you didn't believe in me," Zootfrog said, giving him a look. "Anyway, it's your sister's call. Come on, Ainsley, hit me."

"You want me to punch you?" Ainsley asked, genuinely shocked.

"No, I meant 'hit me' as a figure of speech. Hit me with your wish."

"Oh, right, sorry." Ainsley was a little embarrassed. "Well, OK. I wish our dad had a brand-new also-mom to love him forever and to love us and to make him stop moping and playing sad music."

Zootfrog was silent for a long time. She flew into the branches of the tree and sat, head in hands, thinking. Then she zoomed back to the kids, who were staring hopefully at her. She cocked her head and looked at them.

"You were right," Zootfrog said finally. "That's a biggie. Maybe I was a little hasty taking the pony offer off the table."

"I'm sorry," Ainsley said. "I don't need a pony, but Dad does need an also-mom."

"OK, let's go through it. We're talking about an also-mom. Love forever. No more sad music. There's actually a few wishes in there, not just one."

"We don't mind if Dad plays the sad music as long as he doesn't get that look on his face," Ainsley said.

"It's got to be somebody he's known for a long time, so that she knows what he's like, and it won't go wrong if she discovers that he eats grilled avocado-and-tofu sandwiches for breakfast," Harlan said.

"It's got to be someone who likes kids and likes the beach and is into sports and thinks Dad's jokes are funny," Ainsley added.

"It would be perfect if this person were just as lonely as Dad, so that she'd be as happy as him when they meet up and fall in love. Maybe she should come from another city, where she feels strangely alone although she's surrounded by people," Harlan said.

"I'm not sure about that last part," Ainsley said. "I'd be happy with somebody from across the street — but not Miss Tractorcrank. She's horrible."

Zootfrog nodded. She could see that their minds were made up. From somewhere in a pocket inside her golden tunic she produced a calculator and started tapping the keys. "Also-mom times forever. Carry the seven, divide by two homes, add sad music, and multiply by two kids . . ."

Harlan said, "I didn't know frongles carried calculators."

"Trust me, wishes are more complicated than people believe," Zootfrog told him. "All that stuff on Walt Disney where some fairy godmother just waves a wand. As if! Frongles have to work harder than that. This particular wish could require a lot of magic. It's complex from a mathematical, organizational, structural, and textural viewpoint."

"Huh?" said Ainsley.

Zootfrog gave a low whistle as she consulted her calculator. "OK, I make it a wish to the power of a kazillion."

"A kazillion? What's that?" asked Harlan.

"That's up there. A kazillion is one of the biggest numbers there is."

"I thought infinity was the largest number," Harlan said.

"Maybe in the human world. Trust me, after infinity, there's googly, a gazillion, a trawillion, and then a kazillion. After that comes inginity, intwinity, and, finally, schplock."

"Schplock?" said Harlan.

"Schplock," said Zootfrog.

Ainsley couldn't care less about schplock. "You're not going to grant it, are you?"

"It's not about granting. It's about whether I can actually deliver a wish that big. See, once you get to wishes in the kazillions, it's a matter of *earning* the wish, not just being handed it."

Harlan and Ainsley stared at the floating golden figure.

"Earning it?" Harlan repeated.

"We'll do anything. Just tell us what," Ainsley blurted.

"You're sure?" Zootfrog asked. "It will be difficult."

"We'll do it," Ainsley said.

"It will be disturbing," said Zootfrog.

"We'll do it," said Ainsley.

"It will be very dangerous," Zootfrog warned.

"OK, forget about it," said Harlan.

"No," Ainsley said. "My brother didn't mean that. We'll do it."

Zootfrog flew a little bit away from them, raised her hands, muttered some quiet magic words, and *kapoom!* She was holding a piece of paper.

"Here," she said quietly. "The best of luck. I know how much this means to you both."

Ainsley and Harlan huddled around the paper.

Ainsley said, "It's a poem."

Harlan read it aloud.

> **"If a Kazillion Wish**
> **Is what you would find,**
> **Take 1,000 chocolates**
> **To the Chocolion.**
> **You must seek the One**
> **Who Moves the Stars,**
> **Then consult those men**
> **Who come from Mars.**
> **You must meet the one**
> **Who scares the dark,**
> **And demand a word**
> **From the Lord of Bark.**
> **You must help our friends**
> **Who cut the foam,**
> **And talk to those**
> **Who dreamward roam.**
> **Then a Kazillion Wish**
> **Shall be yours**
> **As long as noble**
> **Be your cause."**

Harlan and Ainsley stared at the poem.

"Well, that's about it for me," said Zootfrog. "Good luck with your quest. Missing you already."

"But . . . ," said Harlan.

"Umm . . . ," said Ainsley.

"What?" Zootfrog was warming up her wings.

"It's just that we have no idea where to start," Harlan explained.

"The poem is very clear. Just follow it."

"But we don't know what it means. We'll never get the wish," Ainsley said.

Zootfrog frowned at them. "Hmm, sometimes I forget how little humans know. You're right, I guess. If nothing else, you'd be eaten by the Chocolion, for sure."

"Eaten?" Harlan gasped.

"Oh, at least." Suddenly, Zootfrog grinned. "I've got it! I know what you need. I'll organize a Bow to guide you."

Ainsley was having trouble keeping up with this conversation. "A bow? Like a bow and arrow?"

"No, not that sort of bow."

"A bow, as in a bow tied in a ribbon?"

"No, a completely different bow."

"Bowwow . . . like a dog barking?"

"Now you're just being silly," Zootfrog said, pulling out her cell phone.

As she dialed, Harlan said, "I didn't know frongles had cell phones."

"No offense, Harlan," said Zootfrog, "but I think

there's a lot of things about frongles that you don't know. Like what color underwear we prefer, for example."

Harlan looked at Zootfrog, decked head to toe in shimmering gold. "Um, gold?"

"That was just a lucky guess," Zootfrog replied. Then into the phone, she said, "Hi, it's Zootfrog from Fruitfly Bay here. I need a Bow to assist with a particularly tricky but very important wish."

Harlan and Ainsley stood by silently as Zootfrog talked into the phone. "Yes . . . Uh-huh . . . It's in the vicinity of a kazillion. . . . Yes, I know. . . . That's right, a kazillion. . . . It's a request for an also-mom. . . . Forever . . . Yes . . . There's got to be somebody else available. . . . You're kidding. . . . Where are they all? . . . And he's the only option? . . . For how long? . . . No, I don't think these kids can wait that long. . . . Oh dear, well, I guess he's going to have to do. All right, I'll turn my locator on now. . . . Thanks for your help. Good-bye."

Zootfrog sighed deeply and stared at the ground.

Harlan said, "Is everything OK, Zootfrog?"

The frongle suddenly straightened up and beamed at them. "Oh yes, just fantastic! You're getting the very, very, very best Bow on the planet to help you with your quest."

"We're on a quest?" said Ainsley.

"I'm not convinced about the Bow," said Harlan.

"Well, you get what you get." Zootfrog shrugged. "I've got to fly. Keep an eye out for a rainbow, and that's your man."

"A rainbow?" said Ainsley.

"That's how Bows travel between their world and ours." The frongle shrugged. "Whenever you see a rainbow, it means a Bow is either traveling up or coming down. When they come down, it's like a slide."

"Don't they crash at the bottom?" asked Harlan.

"You know how people say there's a pot of gold at the bottom of a rainbow? Well, it's actually a sandbox — to break the Bow's fall."

"But what is a Bow?" Ainsley wanted to know.

"You'll find out soon enough. I can see the rainbow forming right now," said Zootfrog. "Like I said, I'm out of here. I have to go keep an eye on the fishface. Good luck, kids."

"Thanks for everything, Zootfrog!" the kids yelled as the frongle became a golden streak, heading off into the sky.

And then they turned their attention to the rainbow, which was clearly beginning to form right next to the picnic area, less than 50 yards away.

4

The Bow

The rainbow grew and grew, stretching to the other side of the sandy shore. The colors became brighter, and Harlan could make out a patch of sand at the closest end.

Suddenly, the air was split by a loud yell. It sounded a lot like *Wheeeeeeeeeeeeeeeeeeee!*

A figure flashed down the rainbow and landed with a soft thud in the sand. It bounced to its feet, brushed down its bright green jacket and even brighter orange pants. It was only about 3 feet tall with skinny legs and a potbelly. Its hair was totally, utterly blue. It straightened the purple cap on its head and finally noticed the two kids standing nearby.

Harlan and Ainsley stared, their mouths hanging open.

"Hello!" said the Bow, in an outrageous and completely unnecessary French accent. "Is zis Fruitfly Bay?"

"Yes," Harlan said.

"*Zee* Fruitfly Bay?" asked the Bow, accent stronger than before.

"Um, yes," said Ainsley.

The Bow looked excited. "Home of the Annual Country-and-Western Trombone Jamboree for Tigers, Monkeys, Porcupines, Elves, Gnomes, and Bows?" he shrieked in his crazy accent, bouncing up and down.

"Um . . . no, I don't think so," said Ainsley.

The Bow smiled. "Well, zat's a relief. If it had been, it would have *freaked me right out!*"

"Are you a strange frongle person, too?" asked Harlan.

"No, I am a Bow, and I'd thank you to remember it, silly human person."

"You're the Bow?" Ainsley gasped.

"Indeed I am. Allow me to introduce myself," it said, bowing low to the ground.

Suddenly, it stood up as tall as it could (not very), smiled a smile that was a mouthful of shiny white teeth, and yelled loudly, "Helllllllllooooooo!"

It opened its arms wide. "It is me. . . . I am me. . . . Me is I. . . . I is it. It is . . . umm . . . ha-ha-ha-ha! Yes, prepare to meet zee one, zee only, zee magnificent, glorious, truly spectacular presence that is . . ."

The kids leaned forward, holding their breath.

"Zat is . . ." He paused for even more dramatic effect, if that was humanly or Bowishly possible. . . . "ZUCCHINI SPACESTATION!"

Ainsley started to laugh. "Zucchini Spacestation?"

"Yes, that is my name and my name is that. Z is for Zoo. U is for Ugly. C is for Carrots. Another C is for, uh,

Cars. H is for Handbag. I is for . . . look, you get zee idea. Zucchini Spacestation is my name and such it is. Nice to meet you. Hello, hello, hello. Ha-ha-ha-ha-ha-ha-ha!"

"Ha-ha-ha-ha-ha-ha-ha what?" asked Harlan.

"Just, ha-ha-ha-ha-ha-ha-ha! You know, as in, 'ha-ha, zis is great!'"

They all stared at one another before Zucchini suddenly yelled again, "And you are?"

Harlan and Ainsley blinked at the little person. Finally, Harlan said, "Well, my name is Harlan. . . ."

"Harlan, Harlan, rhymes with marlin. Zat's a fish!" Zucchini said.

"And this is my sister, Ainsley."

"Ainsley, Ainsley . . . rhymes with . . . actually, Ainsley doesn't rhyme with anything."

"Yes it does," said Ainsley, sounding a little annoyed. "It rhymes with brainsy, sort of."

"Brainsy? Ainsley? Ainsley? Brainsy? Brainsley? Hmmm, I don't think so. Well, whatever! And your last name is . . . ?"

"Banana," said Harlan, regretting it the moment he said it.

"Banana . . . *just like a lemon*!" said the Bow.

"What? A banana is nothing like a lemon," said Ainsley.

"Yellow, fruity, bendy, and good to juggle. I say your father is a lemon!"

"He couldn't be further from it. He's a Banana, and anyway, it's hard to juggle bananas," said Harlan.

"Says you. I believe you have a wish."

And so they told Zucchini about their wish, and how they had to find an also-mom, but Zootfrog said it was a Kazillion Wish, and they were on a quest and had to pass a whole bunch of challenges that were set out in the poem.

"And the first challenge is something called the Chocolion," said Ainsley.

Zucchini leaped to his feet and then realized he was already on his feet and didn't need to leap anywhere. "The Chocolion? OK, I'm out! Good luck."

"What?" cried Harlan and Ainsley.

"Trust me, zee Chocolion is not to be messed with. If you don't give him exactly one thousand pieces of chocolate, he eats you. Where's my rainbow? I'm going up!"

"But you can't leave us," said Ainsley.

"Yep, I can. Bye-eeeee," said Zucchini, packing a suitcase that had appeared from nowhere.

"No, Zucchini, honestly, we need you," said Ainsley.

"You *need* me," said the Bow, pausing from folding giant white underwear into the suitcase.

"Yes, we need you," said Ainsley.

Harlan took a deep breath. "Listen, Mr. Spacestation, this isn't easy for me to say because I didn't even believe in frongles or Bows until about thirty minutes ago, but Zootfrog said you were our only chance."

"Zootfrog said zat? About me?"

"Yes."

"You're not just saying zat?"

"No, we promise," said Harlan.

"Your only chance. Your only hope. Your one shot. Me. Zucchini Spacestation. Zee hopes of a nation riding on my skinny yet strangely heroic shoulders!"

"Well, maybe not the whole country . . . just Ainsley and me," said Harlan.

Zucchini looked suddenly embarrassed and a little moist around the eyes. "You see, zee thing is, nobody has ever needed me before. Nobody has ever even wanted me before and needing is a lot more important than wanting. I don't know what to say."

"How about saying you'll help us?" Harlan said.

"You're right!" Zucchini declared, accent more French than ever. "It eez a quest. An outrageous, dangerous, heroic, tragic, crazy, zany, wild, and once-in-a-lifetime quest!"

"Tragic?" asked Harlan.

"Did I say tragic? I meant to say lawn mower."

"Lawn mower? That doesn't make any sense," Ainsley said.

"Details, details . . . We stand around talking about mowing zee lawn when we should be on our way to the Chocolion! We must ride, at once, to the Liondom."

Zucchini whistled once sharply. Suddenly, three giant pelicans appeared over the trees near the beach. They settled next to Zucchini and he leaped onto the leader's back.

"Hop aboard. Zay don't bite. They're pelicans. Actually, they could fit both of you into their giant beaks without blinking, but try not to think about it," he said.

The kids looked at each other, eyes wide.

"Listen," Harlan said. "Ainsley, we should think about this. There might be another way to get an also-mom. This whole quest thing sounds dangerous and uncertain. We don't know what might be waiting for us. I'm not saying we don't do it. I just think we should sleep on it for a night and possibly draw up a list of alternative options. A quest is not something to be rushed into."

Ainsley climbed onto the back of one of the giant pelicans. "Harlan, I know you like to take time to get your head around things, but sometimes you just have to go and get what you want. Especially when it's something as important as this. I say we do it . . . for Dad."

"Yeah, OK. You're right." He climbed aboard the last pelican. "For Dad."

Harlan's pelican turned its head almost right around and fixed Harlan with a long, cool gaze. Then the pelican winked and spread its wings.

"To the Liondom, stopping only to grab one thousand

pieces of chocolate," cried Zucchini, riding proudly on the front pelican.

Harlan and Ainsley clung on tight as they lifted into the air. Ainsley's heart was thumping as the ground moved farther and farther away, and she could feel her legs trembling against the pelican's feathers. She buried her face into the soft down of the giant bird's neck. One thing was for sure, the day hadn't turned out to be boring.

5

Your Chocolate
or Your Life

They flew and flew, for what seemed like hours. Finally, Ainsley lifted her head out of the soft feathers of her pelican's neck.

"How long have we been flying?" she asked.

Zucchini was leaning back on his bird, with his feet up, reading a magazine. "Almost three minutes," he said.

"Are we there yet?" asked Harlan.

"No," said Zucchini.

"Are we there yet?" asked Harlan.

"No," said Zucchini.

"Are we there yet?" asked Harlan.

"No," said Zucchini.

"Are we there yet?" asked Harlan.

"I could have zee pelican throw you off zee side," Zucchini said.

"Oh, OK . . . sorry," said Harlan. "Are we there yet?"

"Don't start zat again," said Zucchini.

Finally, the pelicans flew closer to the ground, toward a small village on top of a mountain, with rainbows all around it.

"Strictly speaking, I'm not supposed to bring humans here," Zucchini said. "It's a Bow village. But if you don't touch anything and keep quiet, we should be OK."

"What are we doing here?" asked Harlan.

"We have to get chocolate. Remember the poem?

'If a Kazillion Wish
Is what you would find,
Take 1,000 chocolates
To the Chocolion.'

"We need a thousand chocolates, my friend. And zat much chocolate is not easy to come by. Do you have any idea how difficult it is to make, let alone buy, a thousand pieces of the sort of chocolate that the Chocolion demands? You can't just take any chocolate to the Chocolion. It has to be zee best. At zee very least, it has to be frongle chocolate, or Bow chocolate. Ideally, it's cloud chocolate. . . . Chocolate so light and fine zat it exists only in the wisps of actual clouds. Only two or three pieces of such chocolate are found each year. We must find a thousand pieces. Today. Zis minute."

Ainsley was horrified. "It's impossible. What are we going to do?"

Zucchini shrugged. "Ask my cousin. He'll have it."

Harlan blinked. "He will?"

"Sure, my cousin is a chocolate freak. He has buckets of zee stuff around zee house. He'll help."

With that, the pelicans touched down and a small Bow face could be seen peering out the window of the nearest cottage.

The door opened and the Bow yelled, "Zucchini!"

Zucchini spread his arms wide and yelled, "Zanzibar!!!"

"Do all frongles and Bows have names starting with Z?" asked Harlan.

But Zucchini didn't answer. He was charging headlong at Zanzibar, who was running as fast as he could, straight at Zucchini. They were on a high-speed collision course right until the very last second, at which point they collided — *Crash!! Smash!!* — smack into each other, stomach to stomach. Both Bows fell to the ground, sprawled and moaning.

"Are you OK?" Ainsley cried.

"I will be in a moment," Zucchini gasped. "I just have to check that I'm alive."

"What was that?" Harlan asked.

"Traditional Bow greeting," Zanzibar said between whimpers.

"But you almost killed yourselves," Harlan said.

"Yes, by zee age of ten, most Bows choose to live alone. You can see why," Zucchini said.

At last they sat up. "Phew, good to see you, Zanzi. . . . You're as solid as ever."

"You, too, Zucchini. I haven't suffered that much since I greeted Great Uncle Zebrabrain."

"How long were you in the hospital?" Zucchini asked.

"Four months. It was good to see him."

"These Bows are crazy!" said Harlan.

"Says you, humanoid type," said Zanzibar. "Who invented the nuclear bomb, you or us?"

"Good point," said Ainsley.

"Did you miss me, Cousin Zucchini?" asked Zanzibar.

"Like a fish would miss zee ocean, Zanzi. Did you miss me?"

"Like the clouds would miss the sky," Zanzibar said.

"We Bows like to make a big deal of being apart," whispered Zucchini with a grin.

Twenty minutes and ninety-seven cups of Bow tea later, everybody needed to go to the bathroom *really badly*. Then they were off again, riding on the pelicans, loaded up with a thousand pieces of cloud chocolate in a very large sack.

They flew over mountains. They flew over rivers. They flew over the sea. They flew over rain forests. They flew over penguins. Penguins? They briefly turned around to find out why there were penguins in a rain forest (a penguin school excursion, as it turned out). They kept flying north and finally, they were over the Liondom. Harlan and Ainsley knew they were on the right track because they could hear loud roars and growling sounds all around them.

"Sorry," said Zucchini. "Zat's my stomach. It's been a while since I've eaten."

At last, the pelicans landed in the middle of a dense forest. Harlan and Ainsley huddled together while Zucchini gave the pelicans buckets full of fish, which he somehow produced out of a coat pocket.

"OK, pelican birdlike creatures," the Bow shrieked. "I'll whistle as soon as we've seen zee Chocolion."

The pelicans gave the children a sad look, and one of them gently rested his head on Ainsley's chest. Then they flew away.

"Why do I get the feeling that sad looks and gently resting heads are not the pelican way of saying 'Have a great time and relax, you'll be fine'?" said Harlan.

"Well, they're assuming zat you'll be eaten. Nine out of ten people who visit zee Chocolion don't come back." Zucchini shrugged.

Ainsley shuddered.

Zucchini gave her a slap on the back that almost knocked her over. "Cheer up, toots. I said nine out of ten get eaten, but there are three of us. If we assume zee last seven people were eaten, then zat means there are only two of the ten to go. Got it? In other words, we've each got a thirty-three-and-one-third percent chance of *not* being messily devoured. Feel better?"

Ainsley groaned, but quietly, in case Zucchini kept trying to cheer her up.

The Liondom spread out in all directions. A twisted green forest of trees and vines and leaves and palms and fronds and other words that mean "wild jungle," completely surrounded the patch of ground where the three adventurers stood, accompanied only by a large sack of cloud chocolate.

"OK," said Harlan. "We need to think about this. I wonder how we find the Chocolion."

"Well, we could follow the signs." Ainsley pointed to a giant sign with bright neon lights that read: CHOCOLION: THIS WAY!

"How did I miss that?" said Harlan.

"It doesn't really matter." Zucchini shrugged. "Everybody knows zat zee Chocolion finds you!"

Sure enough, just then, the ground shook and they all heard heavy paw-steps in the forest, off to their right. A low, dangerous-sounding growl filled the air.

"Zu-Zu-Zucchini, was that your stomach again?" asked Ainsley.

"N-n-n-no, I'm afraid not," whispered the Bow.

The growl came again, closer this time and sounding unmistakably lionlike. Then there was a roar, like nothing the children had ever heard before. It was so loud that it shook them to their bones. Zucchini put an arm around each of them and pulled them close.

"OK, it's showtime. This is what happens, according to zee terms and conditions of Kazillion Wish quests, as clearly set out in zee paperwork — if you'd bothered to read it back at the Fruitfly Bay picnic area. Zee Chocolion finds you, but only up to a point. He then waits for you to approach him, to make your official request. If you follow zee path, it will lead straight to him. Try to appear friendly and don't make any sudden moves. Keep your hands where he can see them at all times and don't, whatever you do — zis is *ultra* important, so pay attention — do *not* try to get him to sit on a whoopee cushion. Chocolions hate practical jokes."

"What if he doesn't like our request?" asked Harlan.

"Then he eats you," said Zucchini.

"What if he doesn't understand our request?"

"He eats you."

"What if he does like our request but is too busy to help us?"

"Chompy, chompy, chomp," said Zucchini.

"You're not exactly helping our nerves, Zucchini!" Harlan said.

"Sorry. I thought I was being helpful. I didn't even mention zat zee Chocolion's teeth are sharper than any knife ever invented and longer than a sword."

Ainsley trembled from head to toe. "I'm scared!"

"Of course you are, Ainsley. But think of it this way: You're only going to stand face-to-face with a giant lion zat might eat you."

Ainsley groaned.

"Hmm, I've got to work on my motivational speeches," said Zucchini.

"Why aren't you coming with us?"

"Someone has to guard zee chocolate. There are other creatures in this forest and zee last thing we want is for you to lead the Chocolion back here, only to find some monkey has stolen his bounty."

Harlan and Ainsley looked at each other. Their faces

were white, bordering on green, and it wasn't because of all the lush vegetation surrounding them.

"Well, if we're going to do it, we'd better do it now. For Dad," said Ainsley.

"For Dad," said Harlan.

They walked along the path, toward the Chocolion.

Zucchini was left all on his own. Suddenly, he felt very small and very exposed. He huddled down next to the chocolate sack, so that he was half hidden in its folds, wondering if he'd ever see Harlan and Ainsley again. He was sure he would. They were sweet kids, and they had a noble cause.

The smell of chocolate drifted out of the bag, and Zucchini's stomach growled. Surely, the Chocolion wouldn't notice the difference between a thousand chocolates and nine hundred ninety-nine chocolates? Just having one couldn't hurt, could it?

The Bow stuck a hand into the bag and pulled out one wispy, gorgeous, delicious-smelling strand of cloud chocolate. It dissolved in his mouth so beautifully that he thought he might float away. Yum!

Harlan and Ainsley had been gone a while. Maybe the Chocolion had eaten them after all. . . . In which case he wouldn't be coming for the chocolate, or if he did, Zucchini would have to make a run for it and that would be hard on such an empty tummy. Maybe just one more. He had another piece of the chocolate. It really was spectacularly good.

Meanwhile, Harlan and Ainsley walked carefully and quietly along the path. At first it was so thin that they had to walk in single file, brushing branches and giant palm leaves out of their way. But then the path became wider and they were able to walk together, holding hands.

"Harlan, I'm terrified," said Ainsley.

"Look on the bright side. You'll get to talk to a cat — a *big* sort of cat — so you've achieved a wish."

"I didn't mean a lion sort of cat. I didn't mean anything this frightening at all."

"This is the bravest thing we've ever done," said Harlan. "Braver even than that time we had to have measles shots."

"At least we got to eat lollipops then. We didn't get eaten."

"True, but if this goes well, Dad gets an also-mom."

"You're right. We have a noble cause."

Just then, the path turned to the left and the kids stopped dead. Even though their imaginations had been working overtime wondering about the Chocolion, nothing, absolutely nothing, could have prepared them for this.

They were standing in a small roofless waiting room. An enormous orangutan in a smart blue suit was sitting at a wooden desk. There was a small sign on the wall that read: THE CHOCOLION IS IN.

Another sign on the wall read: YOU DON'T HAVE TO BE CRAZY TO WORK HERE, BUT IT HELPS. Hidden speakers were playing a bagpipe version of "The Macarena."

There was also a large door, which was closed. It looked as though it was made of very solid wood.

It had giant metal hinges and a massive door handle that featured long scratch marks on the wood above and below it, as though, just maybe, huge claws had scraped against the wood.

None of this was what Harlan or Ainsley had been expecting.

"Can I help you?" asked the orangutan. "Or do you plan to spend the day gawking and standing there like children who deserve to be eaten?"

"We're here to see the Chocolion," Harlan said.

"Well, of course you are. Do you have an appointment?" The orangutan tapped at a computer and squinted at the screen.

"Um, no . . . We didn't realize we needed one."

"Well, guess what? You don't. That was just my little joke."

"Oh," said Harlan faintly.

Suddenly, the orangutan stood up, walked over to the door, and thumped it with a hairy fist. "Hey, Choco! Visitors."

The door opened.

And the Chocolion appeared.

To say he was huge would be like saying that planet Earth is pretty big. To say he was gigantic would be like saying there are quite a few stars in the sky.

He stood so tall that he would have blocked out the sun if the jungle hadn't already done that. Next to the Chocolion, the orangutan looked tiny (and it was at least three times as big as Harlan!). The Chocolion had a magnificent mane that framed its enormous face.

His eyes, which were deep, deep green, seemed to bore into their very souls.

The creature growled quietly in the back of his throat, and the jungle rumbled all around them.

Ainsley somehow found her voice. "Mr. Chocolion, hello. My name is Ainsley Banana. This is my brother, Harlan. Um, please don't eat us."

The Chocolion looked at them for a long time, then spoke in a deep rumbling voice. "You came all this way to ask that I don't eat you? That's a strange request. I may have to eat you."

"No!" said Ainsley, holding Harlan's hand very tightly. "We came because we asked Zootfrog the frongle for a Kazillion Wish, and we need your help."

"Hmm, Zootfrog, eh? A Kazillion Wish?" said the Chocolion. "And what is your wish?"

"Our father is very lonely. He and Mom don't live together anymore and he listens to sad songs all night. We wished for an also-mom so that he can have somebody to love and keep him company forever."

"Well, that does seem like quite a noble wish," said the Chocolion. "There is only one problem . . . which I'm afraid means I may have to eat you."

"A problem?" whispered Harlan, terrified.

"Yes," said the lion. "I don't see any chocolate."

"Oh," Ainsley said. "We have a thousand pieces back in the clearing at the end of this path, being guarded by Zucchini."

"You left a small green vegetable guarding your chocolate?"

"No, Zucchini is a Bow. Zootfrog asked him to help us."

"A Bow, eh?" said the Chocolion, raising one massive eyebrow. "What kind of chocolate is it?"

"Cloud chocolate, Mr. Chocolion, sir," said Harlan.

"Mmmmm, my favorite. Lead me to it."

So the children headed back along the path, occasionally glancing at each other hopefully but always aware of the giant paw-steps right behind them. Sometimes they could even feel the Chocolion's hot breath on the backs of their necks.

The path became narrow again and they ducked and weaved through the plants until they came to the clearing. They moved sideways so that the Chocolion could stand next to them. But all there was to see was Zucchini Spacestation with a bulging stomach, accompanied by a completely empty sack.

Zucchini looked back at them and burped.

"*Excusez-moi,*" he said.

The Chocolion turned its enormous head toward Harlan and Ainsley and let out an angry growl so loud that it shook the trees to their roots. "What is this? Where is my chocolate? You promised me chocolate! I think it's time you two naughty children were eaten."

"There!" Harlan pointed at Zucchini. "The Bow is made of chocolate!"

"What? What? What what what what what? Hey, wait a minute!" Zucchini said. He looked at Harlan, then looked at the Chocolion, then looked at his stomach. "Uh-oh."

The Chocolion leaped toward Zucchini, but the Bow moved faster than the kids had ever seen anything move before. Zucchini all but flew up the trunk of the nearest giant tree and perched in a branch, out of the angry lion's reach.

"You can't escape, little Bow. I can reach you in two bounds and you know it," growled the Chocolion. "As soon as I've eaten your companions, I'm coming for you."

"Wait!" yelled Zucchini. "It's not their fault. Zay brought you a thousand pieces of cloud chocolate. I got hungry."

"Well, now *I'm* hungry," roared the lion. "VERY HUNGRY."

Harlan and Ainsley huddled together, unable to speak or move.

The Chocolion turned toward them. All they could see were his burning eyes and his giant, terrible, razor-sharp teeth. This was it. He was going to eat them for sure. Ainsley looked around desperately for a weapon or an escape route. But there was nothing.

And then, with his back to Zucchini, the Chocolion unmistakably winked.

"Make your screams sound good," the lion whispered in a remarkably soft voice. "OK?" He smiled at them and winked again.

"OK," they said together, more confused than ever.

Swinging his huge head toward Zucchini, the lion roared. "This is your last chance, Bow. Do you have the chocolate or do I eat your companions? It's not going to look good if you lead a Kazillion Wish quest, and a noble one at that, straight into the mouth of the Chocolion."

"Can we talk about this?" asked Zucchini from his tree.

"NO!" roared the Chocolion. "So long, kids!"

He leaped at the children, completely covering both of them with his head. However, to their astonishment, he only gave them a gentle lick, which was like having wet sandpaper wiped across their faces. Then he murmured, "Scream!"

So they did. It wasn't hard. They had no idea what was going on. They screamed and screamed and screamed.

Zucchini shrieked, "Wait! I've got your chocolate."

The Chocolion gave them another wink and turned around. "You have? Come here, now!"

It wasn't a request. It was an order.

Trembling, Zucchini came down out of the tree. He stood before the Chocolion and saw the children, standing safely behind his massive body.

"Hey, you didn't even eat them!" he said. "I'm glad, by zee way," he added to Harlan and Ainsley.

"I still might eat them, Bow, but you'd be the appetizer. Now where's my chocolate?"

Zucchini reached into his pocket and started pulling out strands of cloud chocolate. Strand after strand, piece after piece, he filled the bag. It took more than half an hour for him to produce a thousand pieces of perfect, delicious cloud chocolate from all four pockets of his pants and the inside pocket of his jacket.

Harlan couldn't believe it. "If you had a thousand pieces of cloud chocolate, why did we have to go and get a thousand pieces from your cousin Zanzibar?"

Zucchini shrugged. "I thought it would be a blast to see Zanzi."

Ainsley couldn't believe it, either. "Why did you eat all the chocolate in our sack if you had a thousand pieces of your own?"

"Well, why eat your own chocolate if you can scarf down somebody else's?"

"Good point," said the Chocolion. "Even so, Bow. You left that rescue a little late. I *might* have eaten them."

"Yeah, thanks for nothing," grumbled Harlan.

"You should have seen your face," Zucchini said. "It was a picture."

Ainsley turned to the Chocolion, who was sniffing at the bag of chocolate, looking pleased.

"Mr. Chocolion? Thank you very much for not eating us."

"That's OK, little one. It's not often that I receive a truly noble request. Thank you for the chocolate and congratulations on being brave enough to seek me out."

"There's only one problem," Harlan said. "We have no idea what's supposed to happen now that we've found you."

"That's easy, Harlan," said the Chocolion. "I give you a word and you continue on your quest, gathering all the other necessary words. If and when you collect all the words, your Kazillion Wish will be granted. And I hope it is. Your father must be a very special man."

"He is," said Ainsley.

"I suppose I'd better write this word down, then," said Zucchini, pulling a huge notebook out of his coat pocket.

"How much stuff do you have in your pockets, exactly?" asked Harlan.

"Sorry . . . a Bow secret," Zucchini said smugly. "OK, Chocolion, I'm ready for zee word. Hit me."

"You want me to punch you? OK," said the Chocolion. He swung a massive paw, knocking Zucchini clear over the trees. They heard a loud crash, half a football field away.

The children stared at the Chocolion with wide eyes.

"Well, he deserved it, didn't he?" The Chocolion shrugged, before unexpectedly breaking into a fake French accent to mimic, "Oh, you should have seen zee look on your face."

The Bananas rolled around, laughing.

Zucchini staggered back into the clearing. "You know, 'hit me' was a figure of speech," he said.

"Sorry," the Chocolion said. "All right. The word I must give you is 'Here's.'"

"Hears? As in I can hear you?" asked Harlan.

"No, here's. H-E-R-E-apostrophe-S," spelled the Chocolion.

"Zat's two words. You know, it's short for 'here is,'" Zucchini said.

The Chocolion growled softly but with an unmistakably threatening edge.

"No, no, that's good enough for me," said Ainsley. "Our word from the Chocolion is 'Here's' and we're very grateful for it, aren't we, Harlan?"

"We sure are. Thank you, Chocolion. Thank you so much."

Zucchini was bouncing up and down. "Here's. Rhymes with gears, leers, jeers, tears, fears, beers, peers, weirs, years, deers . . ."

The Chocolion growled menacingly again.

"Sorry," said Zucchini.

"As I said, Chocolion. Thank you," Harlan said.

"You're welcome, Harlan," said the Chocolion. "Good luck with your quest. What's next?"

Harlan pulled out the poem and read the next verse:

"You must seek the One
Who Moves the Stars,
Then consult those men
Who come from Mars."

"Ah," chuckled the Chocolion. "Then you're going to meet some very interesting people. . . . Well, one interesting person and some very interesting aliens."

"Aliens?" Ainsley said. "For a moment there, I thought you said 'aliens.'"

"Aliens," said the lion. "Well, eventually. But first you have to visit Macklin."

"Macklin?"

"The One Who Moves the Stars. Your Bow knows where to find him. Good luck. I'll be following your progress."

Ainsley gave the Chocolion the biggest hug she could, which wasn't easy because her arms didn't reach around his neck.

"Thank you again," she said.

"You're welcome, Ainsley," he said. "Say hello to Macklin for me."

And with that, the Chocolion walked back into his forest, just as three shadows from above signaled the arrival of the pelicans.

Zucchini whistled loudly, then danced a little jig. "Well, zat went well," he said.

"Yes . . . after you nearly got us *eaten!*" Harlan pointed out.

"Oh, come on. . . . I was just fooling around. We're all here, aren't we? Safe and sound, not lost but found, whole and round, whole and zound, zound and flound, glound and glound." He was bobbing up and down. "Chound, wound, kound, dound, quound, nound, hound. Hey, hound! Like a dog!"

"You forgot *pound* into the *ground!*" yelled Ainsley, and charged the Bow, knocking him clean over and wrestling him to the forest floor. Harlan had to drag his furious little sister away from Zucchini, who was yelping and laughing at the same time.

"Hey, Ainsley, you gave me a Bow greeting! I'm honored."

Ainsley took some deep breaths and shook her head. "You are crazy."

The Bow bowed low. "Why, thank you."

"Where is this Macklin person?" asked Harlan.

"It's a long flight. We have to head to the Starry Eye Café."

"Where's that?" asked Harlan, climbing onto his pelican.

Zucchini paused for dramatic effect. . . . "It can be found . . . in my pants!"

"WHAT?" yelled Ainsley and Harlan together.

"OK, I lied. It's south. Let's go."

And they flew away, leaving the Chocolion and his jungle far below.

6

Macklin and Milk Shakes

The pelicans flew over rivers, over farmland, over the sea, over giraffes.

"Hang on a second!" Harlan yelled. "There aren't any giraffes in the sea."

"Maybe zay were sea horses with realllllly long necks!" Zucchini was doing a handstand on his pelican's back.

"I'll give you a long neck if you're not careful," said Ainsley.

They flew on and on and on.

"Zucchini, how much farther is it?" asked Ainsley.

Zucchini scratched his head. "Well, it's more than one mile, but less than a million."

"Hey, that doesn't help!" said Harlan. "It could be anywhere up to a million miles away."

"Well, zee number twelve is in there." Zucchini looked shifty.

"So it's twelve miles?" Ainsley asked.

"I didn't say zat . . . you did."

Harlan looked at Ainsley who looked at Zucchini who looked at Ainsley who looked at Harlan who looked at Zucchini.

"What's the big secret?" asked Harlan.

Zucchini thought about it and smiled, revealing a mouthful of shiny white teeth. "Secrets are fun!"

Exactly 12 miles later, the pelicans landed at a seaside town outside a small building next to a pier. The building had arched windows and a domed roof. A sign, with lights making up the letters, said: THE STARRY EYE CAFÉ.

Zucchini pulled fish, an octopus, and a large stingray out of his bottomless pockets and gave them to the pelicans, who gulped them down and flapped their wings good-bye as they flew off. The kids waved back until the birds were just three dots in the sky.

Zucchini was already heading for the door of the Starry Eye Café. "Oh boy, oh boy, oh boy," he said. "This place has zee best ladybug milk shakes in zee entire universe!"

Harlan and Ainsley gave each other a look. "Ladybug milk shakes?"

But Zucchini had already rushed through the door.

Harlan and Ainsley were thirsty, so they rushed into the café, right behind the Bow. As soon as they were inside, they stopped and gasped. Not exactly in that order. In fact, they were gasping even before they'd stopped, but you get the idea. The point is that the interior of the Starry Eye Café was enough to make anybody gasp. And stop in their tracks.

Let's start with the furniture. There were more than a dozen tables, all painted in wild colors. Green, red, orange, blue, purple, pink . . . you name it. Turquoise was in there. Yellow. Emerald green. Almost every color you could name could be seen in one of the tables. Even a few colors you probably couldn't name, such as turgreen, blay, or purplange. Ainsley noticed a golden table with blue swirls near the window, while Harlan liked the bright red one with yellow-and-orange flames rising up its legs. One table was decorated to look like craters on the moon and another was painted as though it were a huge block of Swiss cheese, complete with actual holes.

If they thought the tables were impressive, the chairs were jaw-dropping. For a start, they didn't have any legs. They were simply seats and backs that floated at just the right distance below the surface of the multi-colored tables. They, too, were a variety of colors, but first-time visitors to the Starry Eye Café tended to miss the colorful nature of the chairs because they were so worried that a floating chair would drop them on the ground at any second. They shouldn't have worried — these chairs had never let a single person hit the ground; even the day that Great Big Bob Fatman Tubby-tummy had dropped by and drank forty-seven milk shakes. (Although his chair did need a couple of weeks of rest to recover.)

The counter was along the south wall of the café. It featured milk-shake blenders, ice-cream freezers, flavored-topping holders, and a coffee-making machine. One end of the counter was covered in jars filled with marshmallows, gummy worms, Smarties, chocolate chips, and corn chips, as well as wood chips (along with hammers, saws, and nails).

Harlan's attention was drawn to twenty-seven strange levers, running the length of the counter on the western side. Most of the levers were gold or silver and came in a variety of shapes with knobs on top — although two had a half-moon carved into their peaks. Four of the levers were black, one was pure white, and one featured a sculpture of a comet. The levers were at various angles and occasionally moved, ever so slightly, up or down. Harlan had no idea what they were.

Standing behind the bar was a boy of about eight years old. He had sandy blond hair, a big smile, and piercing green eyes. He was wearing a wizard hat, a cloak, a T-shirt, and shorts.

"Hello," he said. "Can I help you?"

"You're dressed like a wizard," said Ainsley. "Do you like Harry Potter?"

"I love Harry Potter, but that's not why I'm dressed like a wizard," said the boy.

"Oh. Do you like *Lord of the Rings* and Gandalf the Grey? Is that why you're dressed like a wizard?" asked Harlan.

"I do like *Lord of the Rings*, but that's not why I'm dressed like a wizard," said the boy.

"Do you like to play dress-up? Is that why you're wearing such a cool costume?" asked Ainsley.

"I do like dressing up, and I agree this is a cool costume, but that's not why I'm dressed like a wizard," said the boy.

"Then why are you dressed like a wizard?" asked Harlan.

"Ahhh, you crazy Banana people! He's dressed as a wizard because he *is* a wizard!" Zucchini laughed. "This is Macklin, zee One Who Moves zee Stars. And it's so good to see you again, Macklin, zat I can hardly speak. How are you?"

"Hello, Zucchini Spacestation. I'm very well, thank you, and I've almost finished the repairs after the last time you and the other Bows came to visit," said Macklin, pointing to the wood chips on the bench.

Zucchini grinned at the kids. "Big party. Lots of Bow greetings. Very messy."

"Do you mind if I ask you a question, Macklin?" asked Ainsley.

"Not at all."

"What are all those levers for?"

"They're how I move the stars."

"You actually move the stars?"

"Uh-huh. I'll show you."

Macklin studied the levers for some time. "What would you like me to move? A star or a planet?"

"A planet," said Harlan. "What about Jupiter?"

"Sure," said Macklin. He grabbed a thick silver lever, the fourth down from the southern end. Slowly he edged it up, up, up, and the lever hummed gently. Then Macklin pushed a big green button on the wall behind him and the roof made a squealing sound.

Harlan and Ainsley couldn't believe their eyes. Where the ceiling had been was now a giant movie screen. Stars and planets appeared across the huge expanse of the projected sky. It was as though the camera was flying away from Earth, with stars streaming past on both sides, top and bottom.

The camera ducked and weaved to avoid some asteroids as Jupiter approached. Then the massive gassy planet filled the screen. As Macklin nudged the lever, concentrating hard, Jupiter began to turn, ever so slowly, and float higher, finally settling half a planet-width above where it had started.

"That's incredible! How do you do that?" asked Harlan. "They never taught us *that* in science classes."

"Magic," said Macklin, toggling the lever until the planet returned to its original position.

"Ah, that would be why we never learned it," said Harlan.

Macklin began adjusting a different lever. "Watch what I can do with Saturn. This is really funny!"

He moved the lever down, then up, then around in a small circle. On the screen, the camera zoomed through space again, until it approached Saturn, with its distinctive rings. The planet began to move downward, then headed up and suddenly spun around, so that its rings wobbled and jumbled around crazily.

Everybody laughed until Macklin stopped jiggling and Saturn settled down, looking giddy, if that's possible for an entire planet. Harlan had on his thinking face.

"But why can you do this, Macklin?" he asked. "What's the point of being able to move the planets?"

"It's not just the planets. I move the stars, too. . . . That's how time works. If I don't move the planets, and the stars, and the moon around Earth and Earth around the sun, then time stands still. Most days, I have them on 'automatic pilot,' but I always keep an eye on them, and sometimes I have to make sure they're all moving in the right directions and time is ticking the way it should."

"You seem awfully young to have such a responsibility," said Ainsley.

"Well, my mom and dad help me sometimes, and I have to go to school on weekdays," Macklin said. "That's when the universe goes feline."

"Huh?" Ainsley was confused.

Just then, the dome of the café was lit up by a

shooting star, zooming from left to right with a bright tail flaring behind it.

"Hey, hey, hey, hey, hey!" said Macklin. He opened a small window behind the counter, revealing a staff of café workers, including chefs, waiters, dishwashers, and three Burmese cats, sitting on stools and pushing and pulling levers like the ones at the counter. "Who let that shooting star go?" he demanded.

"Sorry," said one of the cats, a chocolate Burmese. "My paw slipped."

"Well, be more careful, please, Rico," Macklin said.

"Sorry, boss," said the cat.

"Clumsy cat," hissed the dark brown Burmese cat sitting next to Rico.

"Shut up, Co Co, or I'll tie a knot in your tail," said Rico.

"Ooooh, tough cat!" said the third Burmese.

"Don't you start, Choo Choo, you fluff bucket," said Rico.

"Tail breath!" spat Co Co.

"Mouse brain!" hissed Rico.

"Dog face!" snapped Choo Choo.

"Peace and love, cats," said Macklin, closing the window. "Save your fighting talk for the fishface."

The kids heard a strange sound from behind the window: a gulping, wheezing, hissing, purring cackle. It was the sound of cats laughing.

"What is the fishface?" asked Harlan.

"Oh, nothing. Don't worry about it," said Macklin.

Ainsley's eyes were shining. "Talking cats!"

Macklin gave her a smile. "Would you like to say hello?"

"Yes, please! I'd love to!"

He led her through the door to the kitchen, where the animals sat huddled over their levers.

"Hiya, toots. What's happening?" said Rico.

Ainsley was a little shocked. "Toots? My first ever chat with a cat and he calls me toots!"

"He could have called you Bumpy Brain," Co Co pointed out.

"Or Lumpy Head," added Choo Choo.

"Lumpy head?" said Ainsley.

"OK, Lumpy Head was a little strong. Sorry about that."

Ainsley chatted with the cats for a few minutes.

"Of course many people want to talk with cats. We have such fantastic discussions, you'd be crazy not to want to join in," said Choo Choo.

"Really? What do you talk about?"

"Um, other cats. Sleep. Mice. Food. Sleep. Why we hate dogs. Food. Sleep. . . . That's about it."

Ainsley decided it might be time to get back to the main restaurant. Harlan was talking to Macklin.

"So, do you have a word for us, Macklin?" asked Harlan.

"Oh yes, the Kazillion Wish! Well, I can't just give you the word. You have to earn it," he said.

"Oh no, not another test," groaned Ainsley. "I hope you're not planning to eat us, too."

"No, I've already had some yogurt," said Macklin, looking a little puzzled. "But you still have to earn your word. I'll make it easy, though. Name all the planets in our solar system, starting with the planet nearest the sun."

"Sunspot!" said Zucchini.

Macklin, Harlan, and Ainsley said, "What?"

"Sunspot. A planet close to the sun!"

"Sunspots aren't planets," said Harlan. "They're magnetic regions on the sun's surface."

Ainsley rolled her eyes. "Boy, I can tell that you're going to be a lot of help, Zucchini."

"At least he won't get us almost eaten by a large beast this time," Harlan said.

"Yep, that's definitely an improvement."

Zucchini shook his head. "You know . . . you keep bringing zat up. One little incident with a Chocolion and you never forget. . . ."

Just then, a voice filled the air, singing a song. It was a terrible song, annoying and horribly out of tune. In fact, it sounded a lot like a bad opera song, except for the lyrics.

"Just one more kissssssssss, before you go, my lovvvveeeeee, before you say good-byeeeeeee, before you make me cryyyyyyyyyyy. Just one more kissssssss . . ."

"Uh-oh," said Macklin. He opened the window again and all the café staff and cats peered out at him. "Is that who I think it is?"

"Yep, it's almost time for him to appear, and he's warming up his voice," said Choo Choo.

"Who is it?" asked Ainsley.

"It's the man in the moon," said Macklin, rolling his eyes. "Every other day, he feels the need to sing."

Macklin reached under the counter and pulled out a broom. He held it as high as he could and whacked the ceiling with the broom handle. "Hey, Mooney, zip it!"

The singing stopped, there was a pause, and then a far-off voice said, "Is that you, Macklin? You want me to zip up my pants?"

"No, I want you to zip your lip and stop singing."

"Oh, sorry . . . just getting ready for the stage."

"It's a sky, Mooney, not a stage. Try to remember that. Enjoy your night."

"I will . . . bye-ee."

Macklin turned back to his guests. "Sorry, where were we? It's always pretty busy around here."

Harlan was frowning. "All the planets, from nearest the sun? OK, the first one is Mercury, because that's the hottest. Then I think it might be Earth and Mars . . . but what comes next? I have no idea. Is it Venus? Saturn? Oh man, I think Venus is close to the sun! Umm . . ."

Zucchini was bouncing up and down, but he just shrugged when Harlan looked his way. "Hey, you already know zat we Bows aren't big on zee solar-system thing. Sorry."

Harlan put his head in his hands. "I should have paid more attention in class. . . . Mercury, Earth . . . no! Mercury, Venus, Earth, Mars. But then what . . . ?"

Macklin fiddled with a couple of his levers and watched stars move left and right.

Harlan groaned and slumped into a floating chair. "I can't remember! We're not going to be able to get the second word. I'm really sorry, Ainsley."

But Ainsley was smiling in a very smug way. She said, "My very eager mother just sliced up nine pirates."

"Excuse me?" said Harlan.

"My very excellent mother just sat under nine pines," giggled Ainsley. "My very evil mother just served us nasty pickles."

"Ainsley's lost it," announced Zucchini.

"No, she hasn't," said Macklin, grinning. "You've got your word!"

"They're a way to remember the order of the planets," Ainsley explained. "We learned them in school. Mister Vampire eats my juicy steak using no pepper."

"Mister Vampire eats," repeated Harlan. "Mercury. Venus. Earth."

"My juicy steak," said Ainsley.

"Mars! Jupiter! Saturn!" said Harlan, smiling.

"Using no pepper," yelled Ainsley.

"Ulysses zee Nose Picker!" shrieked Zucchini.

"Uranus. Neptune. Pluto," said Harlan triumphantly.

"Hooray!" said Macklin. "You did it."

"Ainsley, you're a genius," said Harlan, giving his sister a giant hug.

"I didn't even know your mother was a planet," said Zucchini. "She must be enormous!"

"No, Zucchini . . . oh, never mind," said Ainsley. "Can we have our word please, Macklin?"

"For sure. You've earned it. Are you ready?"

"Almost!" declared Zucchini, pulling his massive notebook out of his coat pocket. "Let me see, let me see, let me see. . . . The Chocolion's word — he sent a big hello, by the way, Mackie — zee Chocolion's word was 'Here's.' And your word is . . ."

"The," said Macklin.

"Yes, zee word, we want zee word. What is zee word?" said Zucchini.

"The," said Macklin.

"Come on, Macklin, stop fooling around. What's zee word? Out with it!" said Zucchini.

"The!" said Macklin. "My word is 'THE.'"

"Your word is zee what? Your word is zee law? Your word is zee truth? Your word is your bond?" Zucchini was jumping up and down.

"No, I think Macklin means that the word he has to give us is the actual word 'the' . . . T-H-E," explained Harlan.

"Right on, Harlan," said Macklin.

"Here's the . . ." said Ainsley. "That's what we have so far. I still can't make sense of it."

"You will," said Macklin. "Be patient. You've only just begun. Now, who'd like a snack? All this time and not a single order from my café. Harlan?"

"What can I have?"

"Anything at all."

"Pudding?" asked Harlan.

Macklin dug around under the counter and pulled out a bowl. "Here it is. Ainsley?"

"Fish and chips?"

Macklin dug around again. "No problem! Zucchini?"

"Ladybug milk shake! Ladybug milk shake! Ladybug milk shake!"

Macklin started pouring ingredients into a milk-shake blender.

Harlan and Ainsley looked a little worried. "You're not really making a milk shake out of ladybugs, are you, Macklin?"

Macklin giggled. "Sure I am . . . here go the ladybugs, into the milk shake. . . . No, I'm making an orange milk shake with chocolate chips. It's delicious!"

"A Bow favorite!" Zucchini said happily.

7

Larry and Kelroy

As Macklin made four ladybug milk shakes, Harlan pulled the Kazillion Wish poem from his pocket. "Uh-oh," he said.

"What's wrong?" asked Ainsley.

"The next part of the poem:

> '*You must seek the One*
> *Who Moves the Stars, ...*'

"That's you, Macklin.

> '*Then consult those men*
> *Who come from Mars.*'"

Ainsley gulped. "Oh no . . . aliens! They might be dangerous!"

"Dangerous?" said Macklin, surprised. "The aliens . . . dangerous!"

Macklin and Zucchini burst into fits of laughter and Harlan and Ainsley blinked in confusion. They laughed and laughed and laughed. They collapsed on the floor, they were laughing so hard. They were helpless with laughter. Finally, they stopped, gasping for breath.

"Boy, I laughed so hard I almost wet my pants!" said Macklin.

"Uh-oh, I *did* wet my pants!" said Zucchini, blushing and running off to the bathroom.

"What's so funny?" Ainsley wanted to know.

"Aliens . . . dangerous . . . ," said Macklin, giggling all over again. "Trust me, the aliens you are about to meet are not dangerous at all — well, not intentionally. The only way they would be dangerous is by mistake — they might knock something over or bump into you."

"If you were crazy enough to try to fly in their spaceship with them, *zat* would be pretty dangerous," said Zucchini, reappearing in fresh pants.

"Nobody is that stupid!" said Macklin. "They should be here any —"

There was a loud crashing sound outside the café. The crash went on and on, changing pitch as it went. It sounded as though something had bumped into a ladder that had fallen on some cans of paint that had crashed and smashed into a pile of timber and metal that had then rolled onto some glass and smashed it to pieces.

Macklin stopped mixing milk shakes and listened to the absolute silence that followed all the crashing. Finally, he said, "Larry and Kelroy? Is that you?"

There was silence.

Then some more silence.

And there was more silence.

Followed by silence.

Finally, a strange metallic voice that sounded like a robot said, ". . . Maybe."

"Larry! Kelroy!" said Macklin.

The door opened. If Harlan and Ainsley hadn't already seen so many weird things since Ainsley caught the dandelion and Zootfrog the frongle appeared, this would have been the weirdest thing they'd ever seen. In fact, even after seeing Zootfrog, Zucchini Spacestation, the violence of a Bow greeting, giant pelicans, a desk-bound orangutan, a Chocolion, and movable planets, Larry and Kelroy might STILL have been the weirdest things they'd ever seen.

For starters they were purple. And they had four arms. And five legs. They were wearing striped pants, with strange flipperlike feet sticking out the ends. Apart from their long-sleeve T-shirts — Larry had an L on his, while Kelroy had a K (handy for people trying to tell them apart) — they were identical. As well as all their legs and arms, they had strange hoselike tentacles sticking out of their backs, which floated through the air as though they had minds of their own. The tentacles glowed at the end, with what looked like sparks of electricity, small planets, sonic waves, and other strange things pulsating out of them. Finally, Larry and Kelroy had two antennae sticking out of their heads that hummed gently. Harlan and Ainsley were pretty sure that these two weren't human.

"Hi," said Larry in his metallic voice.

"How ya doing?" said Kelroy in the same metallic voice. "Nice to see you."

"Hello," said Ainsley. "I don't mean to be rude, but what are you?"

"We're Martians," said Larry. "We come from Mars."

"That's a planet," said Kelroy.

"It's not far from here," added Larry.

"You could almost walk. . . . Well, actually, you'd need a spacecraft," Kelroy said.

"Do you know, if you spell 'Mars' backward, it's 'Sram'?" said Larry.

"That's just one of the many interesting facts about Mars," said Kelroy.

"Although not many people bother to spell 'Mars' backward because 'Sram' isn't even a real word," said Larry.

"That wasn't an interesting fact about Mars," commented Kelroy. "That was an interesting fact about Sram."

"You're unlike anybody we've ever met," said Harlan, choosing his words very carefully.

"Why, thank you. Most Martians are green, but we like to think we're special," said Larry.

"Because you are purple?" asked Ainsley.

"Yes," said Kelroy. "Our father accidentally spilled purple paint all over us when we were kids. Martian paint doesn't come off."

"That's terrible!"

"Actually, that was a Martian joke. We Martians have a wonderful sense of humor," said Larry.

"That was another interesting fact about Mars," said Kelroy.

Harlan and Ainsley stared at the Martians, unsure what to say or do next.

"Hey, would you like something to eat?" asked Macklin.

"Why, yes, thank you, Macklin," said Kelroy. "I would certainly enjoy devouring a doughnut."

"We Martians love our doughnuts," said Larry.

"That's just another . . ." began Kelroy.

". . . interesting fact about Mars. Yeah, yeah, yeah," said Zucchini. "Honestly, you're acting as though none of us has ever been to your planet."

Larry and Kelroy stared in amazement at the Bow. "You've been to Mars?"

"Well, no . . . I haven't," said Zucchini.

"These kids have been to Mars?"

"I don't think so. Have you, Harlan? Ainsley?"

Harlan and Ainsley shook their heads.

"Macklin!" said Larry. "You never told us you'd been to Mars."

"That's because I haven't," he replied, placing two doughnuts on a plate.

"Then nobody here *has* been to Mars," said Kelroy.

"My point exactly!" declared Zucchini, which left everybody so confused that nobody was able to speak for a while. Finally, Larry said, "Hey, Harlan and Ainsley! Would you like a ride in our spacecraft?"

Behind the Martians, Zucchini and Macklin shook their heads furiously, Macklin waved his arms and mouthed, "No! No! No! Definitely not!" Zucchini put his head in his hands, still shaking it from side to side.

"Maybe some other time . . . ," said Harlan politely.

"We've got to keep moving . . . to, umm, see a man about a dog," said Ainsley.

"There are dogs on Mars, but they look different from Earth dogs," Larry said sadly.

"That was just another interesting fact about Mars," said Kelroy.

"It's a shame you don't want to ride in our spacecraft because we were going to take you to see our interesting Martian pets," said Larry.

Zucchini was hiding his head in his hands again.

"Oh well, some other time, OK?" said Harlan.

"Also, if you rode in our spacecraft, you would earn the next word for your Kazillion Wish quest," said Kelroy.

"Oh well. Never mind," said Larry.

"No, wait!" cried Ainsley. "We need that word."

"And we'd love to come for a ride in your space-craft," said Harlan.

"You would?" asked Larry and Kelroy together.

"Absolutely," said Harlan, glancing over his shoulder at Macklin and Zucchini. Macklin shrugged and Zucchini fainted.

Several ladybug milk shakes later, Zucchini was back on his feet and everybody was outside the café, staring at the spacecraft that had half landed, half crashed in the parking lot.

"Behold *The Beast*!" declared Larry.

"'Beast' is a good word on our planet," said Kelroy. "It means 'magnificent blue monster.'"

The spacecraft was indeed blue — a very faded blue. It was also very old. Harlan and Ainsley had never seen a genuine spacecraft before, but they could tell that this one was the equivalent of an old Chevy or Ford, way past retirement age. The spacecraft was long and flat with a bench seat in the front and another behind it. There was also a large space like the back of a station wagon. Instead of wheels, the spacecraft had rockets pointing up, and there were wires and hoses and pipes sprouting out all over it. A pair of fluffy dice hung off a rearview mirror, and on the dashboard there was a model of a dog with a nodding head.

"We like to add some cool, hip, and happening touches to our spacecraft," Larry said proudly.

"That was an interesting fact about us," said Kelroy.

The Martians piled into *The Beast*, arranging their multiple arms, tentacles, and legs into the front seat, while Harlan, Ainsley, and a very reluctant Zucchini Spacestation, got into the back, occasionally having to duck away from Martian tentacles that waved randomly about, buzzing and flashing.

The children fastened their seat belts and couldn't help noticing that Zucchini had put on a suit of armor, wrapped himself in pillows, and chained himself to the seat. "Just ready for a nice relaxing ride," he said, his voice muffled by the pillows.

Larry and Kelroy checked the vehicle's instruments, "Steering Frisbee . . . check . . . gear-buzzer . . . check . . . accelerator banana . . ."

"Banana?" said Ainsley.

"Not a member of your family . . . part of our space-ship," explained Larry.

Larry and Kelroy clicked their seat belts and the spacecraft was ready for liftoff. Kelroy pulled out a flower-shaped key, which was kind of weird, and tried to start up the engine.

The engine went *rrrr, rrrrr, rrrrr, rrrrr, rrrrr.*

Nothing happened. Kelroy tried again.

The engine went *rrrr, rrrrr, rrrrr, rrrrr, rrrrr.*

Larry said, "Kelroy, wait! Before we go, I need to go to the restroom."

So Larry got out and raced back into the Starry Eye Café.

When he returned, Kelroy tried starting the engine again.

The engine went *rrrr, rrrrr, rrrrr, rrrrr, rrrrr.*

Kelroy said, "Now I need to go to the restroom."

Kelroy got out and disappeared inside the café, re-emerging a few minutes later. At which point everybody else needed to go to the restroom.

Finally, they were all back in *The Beast*, and Kelroy turned the flower-shaped key once more.

The engine went *rrrr, rrrrr, rrrrr, rrrrr, rrrrr.*

And Larry said, "Uh-oh, I forgot my coloring book."

Everybody groaned and rolled their eyes. Macklin had to run back inside to find the book and, finally, they were ready to go.

The engine went *rrrr, rrrrr, rrrrr, rrrrr, rrrrr.*

The engine went *rrrr, rrrrr, rrrrr, rrrrr, rrrrr* again.

Kelroy said, "I think we're out of gas."

Larry said, "Try once more."

Kelroy turned the key and the engine went *KA-BOOM! The Beast* made a sound like a huge pineapple thudding into jelly, and suddenly, they were screaming through the air faster than an emu being chased by a crazed platypus . . . actually, a lot, lot, lot faster than that.

Harlan's and Ainsley's heads took a while to catch up with their bodies. *"Yaaaaaaaaaaaaaaaaa!"* they both screamed as *The Beast* flashed up through clouds and sky, until Earth was miles below them. Zucchini only beeped occasionally, muttering and whimpering under all his armor and cushions. Larry and Kelroy were busy pushing buttons, turning levers, and busying themselves with other *Beast*-driving activities.

All the time, the spacecraft was traveling straight up — like a rocket heading for deep space.

Until Larry said, "We hope you enjoyed takeoff . . . now we are ready to descend."

At which point Harlan and Ainsley distinctly heard Zucchini say, "Uh-oh."

The Beast stopped, hovered briefly in the air, and then plummeted back toward Earth. Fast!

"Aaaaaaaaaaarrrrrrrrrrggggggggggghhhhhhhh!" screamed the kids.

"Aaaaaaaaaaarrrrrrrrrrggggggggggghhhhhhhh!" agreed Zucchini Spacestation.

"Wheeeeeeeeee," said Larry and Kelroy in their tinny Martian voices.

Earth was coming up fast now, and the kids had no

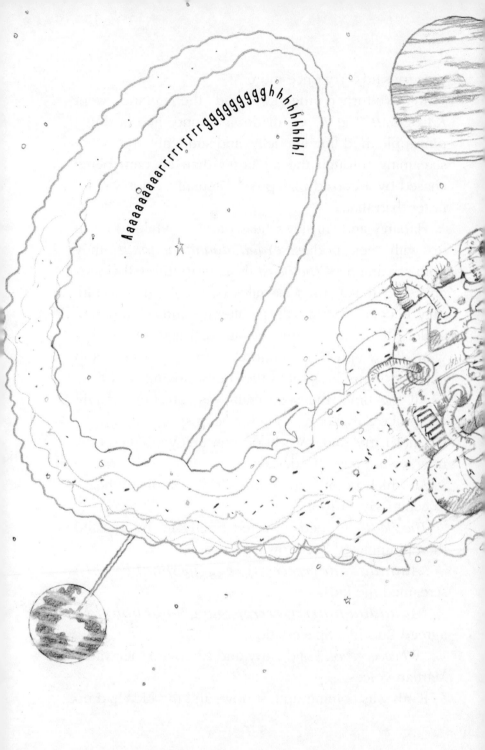

Aaaaaaaaaarrrrrrrgggggggggghhhhhhh!

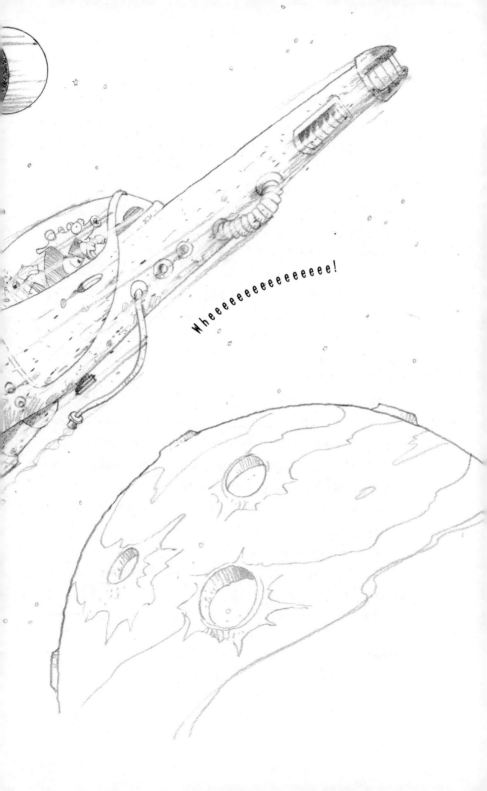

idea where they were going to crash. It looked as if they were falling toward a coastline, but there was also an enormous forest and a few small mountains. "Is this the Chocolion's Liondom?" Harlan yelled above the noise of wind rushing past the plummeting spacecraft.

"I don't think so," said Ainsley.

"Mmmmm, hmmm, ghhmmm, fmmm, mmmm," spluttered Zucchini, having arranged even more cushions and pillows in front of his face.

"What?" Harlan yelled.

Zucchini removed two pillows. "We're heading for zee only Martian kennel on Earth," he said.

"Kennel?" said Ainsley.

"Kennel, and cattery . . . we keep cats there, too. And other Martian animals," said Larry. "We like animals. A lot."

"That was just another interesting fact about Martians," said Kelroy, as Earth screamed up to meet them. Suddenly, Kelroy jammed on the brakes, and landed gently next to a farmhouse.

Harlan and Ainsley scrambled out on wobbly legs.

"Spacecraft travel is fun," said Larry.

"Did you enjoy your flight?" asked Kelroy.

"Ha-have we earned our Kazillion Wish word yet?" gasped Harlan.

"Almost," said Larry. "But first, come and meet our pets."

"Pets! I love pets," said Ainsley.

The Martians waddled over to a woman who had emerged from the farmhouse. She looked almost exactly like a normal Earth grandmother — except for her five legs, four arms, and tentacles. She was wearing a sea-blue dress with small yellow flowers, and she had gray hair.

"Hello, Larry. Hello, Kelroy. I see you still fly like crazy Martians," said the woman in a human voice.

"Hey, we haven't crashed yet!" said Kelroy. "Well, not today, anyway."

The woman saw the Bananas and the Bow standing by *The Beast*. "Hello! My name is Gri Gri," she said.

"Hi, Gri Gri . . . I'm Harlan and this is my sister, Ainsley."

"I hope this isn't a rude question, but are you a Martian or are you from Earth?" asked Ainsley.

"It's a perfectly reasonable question, dear. I'm actually a bit of both. My father was a Martian, but my mother was from Earth."

"Wow!" said Ainsley and Harlan together.

"They met at a party," she explained.

"Gri Gri looks after our pets," said Larry. "Can we see them, please, Gri Gri?"

"Of course, boys." She pulled out a giant key the size of a rolled-up newspaper. "Let's go to the pet house."

The pet house was massive, at least five times bigger than Harlan and Ainsley's home.

"We love our pets," said Kelroy, "but when we go visiting, we leave them with Gri Gri so that they're well taken care of."

"And here they are." Gri Gri opened the pet-house door.

Harlan and Ainsley were ready for anything, given their remarkable experiences already, but they gasped all the same. What they saw was a man with a gray beard, wearing glasses. He was about the same age as Gri Gri.

"Hi, Ronnie," said Larry.

"Hi, Larry," said the man.

Needless to say, this man and that conversation weren't what had made the kids react.

No, they were gasping about something else. Bounding toward the group was a huge, fluffy pile of animal, like nothing they'd ever seen before. It was bright pink and had ten legs. It had giant horns emerging from either side of its twelve eyes, and antennae popping out of the top of an area that the kids assumed must be its head. It made a strange humming noise that was occasionally interrupted by a *honk!* Larry and Kelroy ran toward the creature and gave it a big hug — arms and tentacles flying in all directions.

"This is our dog," said Larry.

"DOG?" Ainsley said.

"Yes, Martian dogs are different from Earth dogs," said Larry a little unnecessarily.

"That was an interesting fact about dogs," said Kelroy, as he was smothered in honks and licks.

"What's its name?" asked Harlan.

"Water Bucket Head," said Larry.

"Of course it is," said Ainsley.

Seconds later, another Martian dog — bright green this time — bounded up.

"And this is Vacuum Cleaner Brain," said Kelroy.

Harlan could only smile as the Martians hugged their pets. However, Zucchini ran as fast as he could out of the shed, then peeked back around the door. He'd seen a duck bigger than any duck anybody had ever seen. Its head was up near the roof and its body filled the whole space. Its webbed feet were about the size of a small car.

"This is our duck, Quack Quack Bric-a-Brac," said Larry.

"And our horse, Jingle Bells Batman Smells," added Kelroy.

Harlan gazed around but couldn't see a horse anywhere.

"Watch out. You almost stepped on him!" cried Larry.

Harlan looked down, and there, no taller than his knee, was a tiny horse, galloping around his feet and neighing in a high-pitched little voice.

"Martian horses are a lot smaller than Earth horses, but our ducks are pretty big," said Larry.

"That was another interesting fact —"

"We know! We know!" said Zucchini, eyeing the massive duck suspiciously.

Finally, the Martian pet-fest was over and everybody headed back to *The Beast*.

"Thanks, Gri Gri. Unless something happens with the fishface, we'll be back for the animals in a few days," said Larry.

"No problem. Ronnie and I like the company," said Gri Gri.

"Did you say fishface?" asked Ainsley.

"No, I think I said boat race," said Larry.

"No, you didn't," said Ainsley.

"First place," said Kelroy.

"Open space," said Larry.

"Amazing grace," said Kelroy.

"The greatest race."

"Back brace."

"Outer space."

"In your face."

"Hmmmm," said Ainsley, who was unconvinced.

"Thanks for showing us your pets, guys. What happens now?" asked Harlan, though he was not sure he really wanted to know.

"We had better give you your word," said Kelroy. "Thank you for flying in our spaceship."

"It was our pleasure, Kelroy. We've had an incredible time," said Ainsley.

"OK, here is your word. Are you ready?"

"You betcha," said Zucchini, who had managed to pull his giant notebook out of one of his coat pockets, despite the fact he was once again bundled up in heavy armor, pillows, cushions, a crash helmet, and wearing a parachute in a backpack. "Let me have it!"

"You want me to punch you?" asked Larry.

"No, I want the word," said Zucchini.

"Oh OK . . . 'thing.'"

"Well, zat's not very polite!" said the Bow.

"Excuse me?" asked Larry.

"Calling me a thing. It's not polite. I'm a Bow, you know."

"I didn't call you a thing."

"Yes, you did. You said, 'Oh OK, thing.' I heard you, you nasty little Martian rude person from Mars."

"No, I said, 'Oh OK . . . thing,'" Larry said.

"Exactly," agreed Kelroy. "That's quite different from 'Oh, OK, thing.'"

Everybody was confused now.

Harlan finally said, "Are you saying that you said, 'Oh, OK,' as in yes, we can have the word, and then you said 'thing'?"

"You're pretty clever for an Earth boy," said Larry.

"So our next word is 'thing,'" said Ainsley.

"Absolutely, completely, totally correct," said Kelroy.

"In that case, the Kazillion Wish words we've collected so far are: 'Here's the thing,'" said Ainsley. "What's the thing?"

"I guess we need more words so we'll know." Harlan shrugged. "We had better keep going with our quest."

"Can we come with you?" asked Larry. "We could give you a lift in our spacecraft."

"I guess so," said Harlan. "If you'd like to."

"It might be fun," said Kelroy. "Where do you have to go next?"

"The Kazillion Wish poem says:

'You must meet the one
Who scares the dark,
And demand a word
From the Lord of Bark.'"

"Uh-oh, it's not going to be fun," said Kelroy.

"Why not?" asked Ainsley.

"Because!" Zucchini suddenly said. "Because we have to visit zee Zone of Darkness. . . . One of zee scariest, most frightening, challenging, daunting, precarious, terrifying, and most difficult-to-see areas you will ever visit."

Harlan and Ainsley gave each other a look.

"It's lucky you have a Bow with you, right?" said Zucchini brightly.

"One word: Chocolion," said Ainsley.

"Hey, that was one thing. . . . How many times have I almost killed you since then?" asked Zucchini.

"Come on, we'll give you a lift," said Larry.

"This gets better and better," muttered Harlan, but then Ainsley held her brother's hand and said, "For Dad."

Harlan smiled at her. "For Dad," he repeated.

They all climbed into *The Beast*, then had to wait for Larry, then Kelroy, then Zucchini to all get out and go to the bathroom. Finally, they blasted off into the sky — toward the dreaded Zone of Darkness.

8

The Zone of Darkness

The Martian spaceship flew steadily east, and with every mile the sky grew darker and darker. The darkness surrounded them on every side. No matter which window Harlan looked out of, he could see nothing but pitch-black.

It got dark. Really dark. So dark that the word that comes to mind is "dark." Or maybe even . . . "darker."

"Where are we?" asked Ainsley.

"My guess would be the Zone of Darkness," said Harlan.

"You're really smart for an Earth kid," said Kelroy.

"Thanks," said Harlan, wondering if that meant Martian kids were smarter or dumber. He thought about asking Zucchini, but the Bow was completely buried in protective gear, even though *The Beast* was now cruising carefully.

Larry peered through the windshield. "You know, Kelroy, it's lucky that we Martians don't get scared."

"Why's that, Larry?" asked Kelroy.

"Because otherwise I'd be pretty scared."

"You know what I like about the dark, Larry?"

"What, Kelroy?"

"The fact that it's so dark."

"It certainly is dark."

From under his pillows, Zucchini whispered to Harlan and Ainsley, "You know, Martian conversations aren't always so great."

The darkness became so intense that even the ship's lights couldn't carve through it, and Kelroy decided he had better land. They touched down in what appeared to be a clearing, but it was hard to tell because it was, in case you haven't picked this up by now . . . dark.

The adventurers emerged from the spaceship and huddled together, squinting in the gloom and trying not to get spooked by the overwhelming blackness all around.

Every now and then, they could sense something moving in the distance or maybe quite close — it was hard to tell. The spookiest thing was the silence. In most situations you would normally hear tree branches scraping, or maybe the wind blowing, or perhaps a bird or a faraway car. But there was absolute silence.

Until Zucchini yelled, "La la la la la, la de la la la!" so loudly that everybody jumped out of their skin . . . well, only Kelroy, who quickly pulled himself back together. "Sorry about that," he said.

"Zucchini!" said Harlan. "You almost gave me a heart attack."

"Just trying to break zee silence," said Zucchini. "Having said zat, maybe we should try to keep zee fact we're here a secret."

"It's a little late now," said Ainsley. She felt like something was stirring in the silent dark, in the echo of Zucchini's outburst. She told herself that she was just imagining things.

For another few minutes, they peered into the blackness wondering how long the night would last.

Finally, Larry whispered, "You know, Kelroy, I'm *really* glad that we Martians don't get scared . . . especially of the dark, because otherwise I'd be terrified!"

Ainsley huddled closer to her brother. "Well, there's no doubt about it, I'm really scared."

"It'll be OK, Ainsley," said Harlan. "Our eyes will adjust to the darkness."

But they didn't. If anything, the darkness closed in even more, becoming so intense that it seemed to pulsate around them. They could feel it on their skin and in their hair, twisting and turning like a giant knot, trapping them in an inky net.

"The darkness feels like it's touching me!" said Ainsley.

"It's definitely closing in," said Harlan.

"Not scared, not scared, not scared," said Larry.

Then, to completely spook them, the darkness actually laughed — a low rumbling laugh, like a roll of quiet thunder, but unmistakably a chuckle. And not a pleasant chuckle. An evil, sinister chuckle, like the bad guy's laugh on *Scooby-Doo*.

"Now I'm *really* freaked out!" shrieked Zucchini.

And then it came. A single, dazzling shaft of light away to the south, streaking toward them. As it got closer, the beam became brighter, and they could actually hear the darkness groan in disappointment as its hold on them began to loosen.

The light grew ever closer, and now they could hear music. It was stirring music, the sort that is played by an orchestra, and it filled the air, instilling excitement and hope.

"Is it a helicopter?" asked Harlan, peering at the light.

"Is it a rocket?" asked Kelroy, blinking his Martian eyes furiously.

"Is it a glowworm?" asked Zucchini.

"A glowworm?" asked Harlan.

"Well . . . a really, really big glowworm," Zucchini suggested.

They all stared at him.

"With wings . . . OK, it's probably not a glowworm." He shrugged.

"Not even close, Bow," came a voice from the center of the light. The music swelled again, reaching a triumphant conclusion. "It is I . . . the scourge of blackness, the protector of travelers in the night, the all-around hero of anybody who's scared of the dark. . . . Yes, you can call me . . .

And with that there was a final crash of cymbals and a
brief but spectacular saxophone solo, careening into a
drumroll. The light flashed so brightly that the darkness,
already shrinking, was sent packing toward the horizon.
There, floating in the air in front of them, was a boy,
aged ten, maybe eleven, dressed in a black outfit with a
bright golden sash running from his left shoulder to his right hip.
He wore golden underpants on the outside of his tights, shining
golden boots, and a gold cape that billowed out behind him.
On his chest, in the middle of the golden sash, was a
lightning-bolt design. All around this amazing figure
glowed dazzling bright white light.

"Hey," Zucchini whispered loudly, nudging Kelroy in the ribs. "He put on his pants before his underpants!"

"That's because he's a superhero, idiot," said Kelroy.

"A superhero?" Harlan blinked. He'd never met a superhero before.

"Yes, indeed," declared the floating boy, white teeth gleaming as he smiled a superhero smile. "My name is William, the one who scares the dark . . . better known as Lightning Rod."

"Hello, Rod, nice to meet you," said Larry.

"No, not Rod . . . William," said the superhero.

"Lightning William?" asked Kelroy.

"No, no, no . . . Lightning Rod."

"That's what I said," complained Larry. "Rod."

"No," sighed the boy, looking a little annoyed. "If you're going to call me Rod, you have to call me Lightning Rod. If not, my alter ego is William."

"Well, it's all very confusing," complained Kelroy. "Let's call him Shazam."

"Or Popeye," said Larry.

"Or Superman."

"Or Batman."

"Or Spider-Man."

"Or Wonder Woman."

"Hey!" yelled the flying hero.

"Or Barbie," said Kelroy.

"I'll go away again. . . . Hey, Dark, they're all yours!" yelled the kid, starting to fly away. His music hastily stirred into action-packed departure music.

"No, please don't go!" yelled Ainsley. "They'll be good. Won't you, Martians?"

William hovered, arms folded. "Are you going to behave, Larry and Kelroy?"

"Yes, Mr. Rod, sir," said Larry.

"Only joking, William," said Kelroy.

The music settled into unobtrusive background noise.

"Hey, William, what's with the music?" asked Harlan.

"It's my theme tune."

"Your theme tune?"

"Yes, it follows me everywhere, ever since I became a superhero. It's really weird, actually. . . . It follows my mood and my actions. When I'm doing heroic deeds, or if I'm enjoying a lighthearted moment, or if I'm relaxing after a hard night of scaring the dark, it's always there."

Zucchini scrunched up his face. "Ewww, what does it play when you go to zee bathroom?"

"Zucchini!" said Ainsley.

"I wish I had a theme tune," said Larry. "Martians never get to have them."

"That's just one of the many interesting facts about . . ." Kelroy began.

"Don't start zat again!" cried the Bow.

"Well, I think it's very cool to have your own theme music," said Ainsley. "And thanks for scaring away the dark, William."

"You're welcome," said William, still floating above the ground. "Lucky I did, too. You wouldn't have wanted to go for a walk to your left."

"Huh?" they all spun around and discovered that they were teetering on the edge of the biggest cliff they had ever seen. It was like one of those cliffs in a Roadrunner cartoon, with the ground so far away that it was hard to make out. The drop was so huge that it was like looking out of the window of a plane, and their toes were hanging right over the edge.

"Ahhhhhhhhhh!" screamed Zucchini.

"Not good, not good, not good," said Larry.

Ainsley and Harlan stood frozen in fear.

And then Kelroy lost his balance. At first, he swayed out over the edge, then he overcorrected and leaned away from the massive drop. But then his body lurched out into the yawning chasm again and despite having five legs planted on the ground, he fell, clean over the edge. It got worse, too. As Kelroy plummeted, his arms and tentacles — which had been drifting around in the background, little planets and shocks and buzzing sounds sparking off the ends — suddenly flew in all directions and managed to hook Larry, Ainsley, and Harlan and drag them off the cliff as well.

They all fell.

Zucchini was left at the top, watching the Martian and human bodies of his friends fall away into space, their screams growing ever fainter. He looked at William, who was genuinely shocked, then he shrugged.

"Oh well, if everybody's doing it . . ." he said, and jumped.

Zucchini fell fast — much faster than everybody

else. Bows, for unknown reasons, plummet quicker than any other creature, except perhaps the little-known bowling-ball snails of Argentina, which are exactly the same size, shape, and weight of a bowling ball. (It's extremely rare for one of these creatures to fall off a cliff, but, boy, when they do, they fall fast.)

The only thing going faster than Zucchini was a streak of light that screamed past him — a dazzle of music in its glowing wake. Lightning Rod grabbed Ainsley by the waist and screeched to a halt, holding her safely in midair.

"Harlan! Save Harlan!" she screamed.

The superhero swooped again, still gripping Ainsley with one arm, and streaked toward Harlan. Ainsley's weight slowed him down, but he finally managed to get one finger under Harlan's T-shirt and stop him talking any further. They were still a dizzying distance from the ground.

Harlan swung in space, and Lightning Rod held firm with his superfinger under the boy's shirt.

"Don't worry, I've got you," said Lightning Rod.

But then Harlan's shirt began to tear. "Rats. I knew I should have worn my new *Simpsons* T-shirt," he cursed.

Lightning Rod's finger was losing its grip as the material tore again. Ainsley tried desperately to reach down to grab her brother, but her arms weren't long enough.

Harlan slipped a little. Then a little more. Any second, he'd be gone.

Suddenly his collar came away and he plunged, screaming, toward the ground. He could see Zucchini, Larry, and Kelroy still falling way below, and if you're not scared by now, I'm running out of ways to convince you that this was a serious situation. Luckily, there was a Bow present.

"You know, there is one way out of zis," Zucchini yelled to Harlan as they fell.

"There is? What is it, Zucchini? Quick, tell me!"

Zucchini gave him a sly smile. "It's a secret."

"A secret?" Harlan screamed. "Why on earth would it be a secret?"

Zucchini grinned. "Because secrets are fun!"

Harlan took a deep breath (which isn't easy when you're plummeting toward sharp rocks far below). "Zucchini, listen. Normally, I'd agree with you. Secrets can be a lot of fun. I love secrets. But now is not one of those times. Now is a time when you should tell me the secret, pronto. What is the one way out of this fall?"

"Well, we could build a parachute out of moth wings!"

"That's your plan?"

"As long as zere are moths around. Have you seen any?"

"If we live through this, Zucchini, I'm going to . . ." Suddenly, Harlan's eyes lit up. "I have a better plan! Zucchini, have you got your cell phone?"

"You bet I have. It's got fancy Bow ringtones, games, text-messaging, e-mail. . . ."

"Give it to me," screamed Harlan.

They continued to plunge toward the ground. Harlan looked around for Lightning Rod. He was still holding Ainsley and clutching what was left of Harlan's collar, as he streaked toward them in a last-ditch rescue attempt.

"Lightning Rod. What's the number for the Starry Eye Café?"

The superhero reeled off the number, and Harlan furiously punched the buttons of the cell phone. It was hard to see because his eyes were streaming from the speed of their fall.

"Strange time for a phone call," said Larry, spinning past.

"Very strange," agreed Kelroy, plummeting toward the ever-rising ground and certain death.

They fell and fell and fell. Meanwhile, Harlan had the phone to his ear. "C'mon, c'mon, pick up," he said.

The phone kept ringing, and the ground loomed toward Zucchini, Larry, and Kelroy, who were falling so fast that their hair was nearly ripped out of their heads.

It continued to ring as giant, jagged rocks and extremely hard-looking boulders came into focus directly below them.

It rang and rang as the rocks and boulders grew bigger and pointier and seemed to fly up to meet their puny bodies.

"Any time you like," shrieked Zucchini.

Suddenly a distant voice said, "Starry Eye Café. Hello?"

"Macklin! Help! Quick!" yelled Harlan.

Harlan felt his heart lurch as the ground came at him so fast that he could barely register the speed. He was too late. There wasn't enough time. He estimated he would smash into the sharp rocks within five seconds. He had one last moment to be glad that his sister was safe, held tight in the arms of Lightning Rod.

Harlan closed his eyes, scrunched up his face, and waited for the collision.

It took him at least ten seconds, maybe fifteen, to realize he was still waiting. Then another ten seconds for his brain to become unconfused enough to consider that maybe, just maybe, he could open his eyes.

Harlan sneaked a peek from under one eyelid and his stomach lurched. He was inches from the jagged and extremely solid rocks. He hung in midair, as though somebody had hit the pause button. He risked a glance to his right, and was astonished to find Larry and Kelroy also hovering just above the ground.

"From here the people look like ants," said Larry.

"They are ants, Larry. We're only inches above the ground," said Kelroy.

"I think I need to go to the bathroom," said Larry.

Harlan looked to his left. Zucchini Spacestation was leaning back in thin air, his feet up and his arms folded behind his head as though he lay in a hammock.

"Exciting, eh?" said Zucchini, beaming at him. "Good going, Harlan. You saved us."

"It — it worked!" said Harlan, when he could organize his mouth to talk. Into the phone, he said, "Macklin?"

"How's tricks, Harlan?"

"I think my tricks are good. I can almost breathe again."

"That was quick thinking. Well done. Say hi to Lightning Rod for me. William's my brother, you know."

"Um, OK. Sure." Harlan hung up, although his hammering heart suggested he wasn't quite ready for family reunions just yet.

Lightning Rod floated down to meet them, holding Ainsley in his arms.

"What happened?" she asked. "You're floating?" Her eyes opened even wider. "Harlan, you're magic, too?"

"Actually, I think he is more brainy than magic," Lightning Rod said. "I think he phoned my brother."

"Your brother?" Ainsley was still trying to catch up.

Harlan smiled. "Macklin. The One Who Moves the Stars. He also controls time, because time is the thing that counts how fast Earth is traveling through space, around the sun. I was hoping he could slow our fall. In fact, he stopped it."

Lightning Rod nodded. "It was a pretty cool trick from young Mack, especially for an eight-year-old."

"You're not wrong," said Harlan, giving Lightning Rod a very serious look. "But listen, even before Macklin saved us, you saved my sister, and I'll never forget it. Thank you."

William looked embarrassed, but very pleased. "Well, saving people is what being a superhero is all about. You didn't do too badly yourself."

"Harlan, you're a genius," said Ainsley. "But how will we get back up the cliff?"

"I'll fly you up to your spaceship," said Lightning Rod. "One by one."

So he did, soaring up and up and up five times, twice with a human child in his arms, twice holding a Martian, and once with a screaming Bow wrapped around his legs, squeezing so hard that William got pins and needles. The whole time, his theme music was playing like crazy in the background, providing a stirring soundtrack for his heroic deeds as he carried his companions through the sky.

At last, they were all standing by *The Beast*.

"You know what?" said Harlan. "I'm hungry."

"I'm thirsty," said Ainsley.

"I'm crazy!" said Zucchini.

"I'm tired," said Kelroy.

"I'm not scared," said Larry.

"I'm tired, too, Kelroy," said Harlan.

"Yes, I'm exhausted," agreed Ainsley.

"I feel like I've been awake for days," said Zucchini.

William smiled. "That's because you've been in the Zone of Darkness. When the darkness descends, it's hard to tell whether it's day or night, or how long you've been awake. Once the light returns, you feel kind of strange because your body is not sure whether you've just stayed awake all night, or maybe night came during the day, or maybe you were supposed to be asleep during the nighttime of a day or awake in the light of nighttime or . . ."

"Aye, aye, aye, we get the idea," said Ainsley, holding her head in her hands.

"But where can we rest? Where can we eat?" asked Harlan. "It's a long way back to the Starry Eye Café."

Suddenly, Zucchini Spacestation leaped into the air, spun on the spot, struck a pose, and tugged on his bow tie. "Ta da da da!" he cried. "Relax, human fruit. You'll see Macklin soon enough."

"Human fruit?" Harlan said.

"Um, sorry . . . Did I say human fruit? I meant to say Banana Boy. . . . Anyway, ta da da da!"

"Ta da da da what?" asked Ainsley.

"I know where we can go. There's food, you know. But not much snow. Zee lights will glow and . . . I don't know, I've run out of rhymes. Oh, I've got it! You'll meet a Bow."

"Zucchini, what in the universe are you talking about?" asked Larry.

"My sister's house. For dinner. We could even stay for zee night," said the Bow. "It's not far."

"Your sister?" said Ainsley.

"A Bow dinner?" said Larry.

"A sleepover?" said Kelroy.

"I might join you," said William.

"What's your sister's name?" asked Harlan. "Let me guess. . . . It will start with a Z. Maybe Zing!"

"Nope," said Zucchini.

"Or Zang?"

"Nope."

"Zongo?"

"Uh-uh."

"Zelda?"

"Not even close."

"Zinc-cream?"

"YES . . . You're completely wrong!" Zucchini nodded.

"Zalada . . . ?"

"Nope."

Harlan sighed. "OK, I give up. What is her name?"

"You'll find out," said Zucchini. "Come on, let's go."

9

Lightning Juice

So they lifted off in *The Beast*, with Lightning Rod flying alongside, and left the Zone of Darkness. As they flew away, they could feel the dark reclaiming the space behind them, but Lightning Rod's theme music barely flickered, keeping up a steady, heroic hum.

Before long, the spacecraft descended to a Bow village that looked a lot like the one where Zanzibar lived, except that this one was buried deep in a valley. All around stood magnificent mountains, some dotted with white, which Harlan thought must mean they were high enough for snow. Either that or mountains could now get dandruff.

The village itself was nestled into the base of one of these enormous peaks, surrounded by banana trees and a river that was fed by a giant waterfall farther up the mountains.

The moment they landed, Zucchini threw off his

armor and pillows, and bounded out of the spacecraft. "IT'S ME!" he yelled.

A female Bow bounced through the open doorway of the nearest cottage and cried, "ZUCCHINI!"

"Zat's right!" he screamed, a little unnecessarily.

"It's absolutely *fantastique* to see you!" Her voice had a high-pitched, fake French accent that was possibly even more outrageous than Zucchini's.

With a whoop, Zucchini charged toward her, and she ran even harder toward Zucchini.

"Oh no! Here comes the traditional Bow greeting!" squealed Ainsley, wanting to hide her eyes. And she should have. The collision was sickening. *Smack!* Both Bows fell to the floor.

"Are you OK, Zucchini?" Harlan asked.

"I'm just checking whether all my body parts are connected," he groaned. "Nice to see you, Sis."

His sister staggered to her feet, gulping for breath and trying not to collapse again. "You, too, Zucchini. Hey, who are your friends?"

Zucchini drew himself up to his full height (not very tall). "I'm leading a Kazillion Wish quest, at the request of zee frongles. My human companions, Harlan and Ainsley Banana, have wished for an also-mom for their father. These two gentlemen, Larry and Kelroy, are from Mars."

"Hey, we're gentlemen!" said Larry.

"Sounds impressive," said Kelroy.

"And finally," said Zucchini, "may I present a genuine superhero, who has just saved our lives — it's zee one, zee only, zee truly spectacular . . ."

"We Bows love introductions," said Zucchini's sister.

Zucchini had built up to a big finish. "Please give a warm welcome to . . . LIGHTNING ROD!"

Lightning Rod's theme music gave him a triumphant fanfare, as the superhero stepped forward and shook hands with Zucchini's sister.

"Hi," he said. "You can call me William."

"Hi, William. Boy, having your own theme music is seriously cool!"

Zucchini was nodding. "Zat's just what I said."

Harlan said, "I'm dying to know your name. We know Zucchini and we met Zanzibar . . . so I've been trying to guess yours. Is it Zootananny?"

"No," she laughed.

"Zickitiwickity?"

"No," she giggled.

"Are you Zigloo?"

She shook her head.

"Zigzag? Zogtie? Zootee-fruitee?"

"Nope, no, and not even close."

"Zoonbuggy? Zofabed? Zangatwang?"

"They're all great names, but zey're not mine. In fact, allow ME to introduce myself." She smiled a smile that might have been even toothier than Zucchini's. She paused and her eyes danced. She stood as tall as she possibly could (not very) and milked every bit of drama out of the moment. Then she yelled, "HA-HA!" Then she paused . . .

"Boy, she really IS Zucchini's sister," whispered Ainsley.

Zucchini's sister paused even longer, so that if the children had been holding their breath, fainting would have been a very real option. Finally, she spread her arms wide and yelled, "Allow me to introduce myself. It is I. I am me. Me is who I am. Yes, it's I and zat means me and zat's an I for an eye in an eye of a me in a . . . hmmm, I seem to have lost my way. Anyway, zee important thing is that it is me! And my name is . . ."

Another pause. The kids rolled their eyes.

"My name is . . . BIKINI SPACESTATION!"

"Bikini!" said Harlan. "I never would have got that!"

"Frankly, I'm a little disappointed," said Larry the Martian.

"*What?*" said Bikini.

"I think Swimsuit sounds better than Bikini."

"Swimsuit Spacestation? Zat's a ridiculous name," said Bikini.

"I like it," said Larry.

Kelroy nodded. "Me, too."

"So, did you miss me, Bikini?" asked Zucchini.

"Like zee sky would miss zee color blue," she replied. "Did you miss me, Zucchini?"

"Like a tree would miss its leaves," Zucchini said, winking at the kids. "Actually, I saw Bikini yesterday."

"You crazy Bows!" said William. "Let's eat. Bikini, we didn't arrive empty-handed. I took the liberty of bringing along some of my extra-special Lightning Juice."

"Lightning Juice?" Harlan asked.

"That's right, Harlan. Special superhero juice! It

tastes just like your favorite fruit juice or vegetable juice," William said, pouring glasses for everybody.

"My favorite is pineapple," said Ainsley.

"Guava," said Harlan, tasting his. "Yum, it is, too!"

"Banana, orange, kiwifruit, and raspberry," said Zucchini, taking a sip. "Yippee!"

"Gherkin and asparagus," said Larry. "Tastes great."

"Slug," said Kelroy. "Yum."

"Slugs aren't fruit!" Bikini said, taking a sip of her mango juice.

"Well, that explains why mine tastes more like lemon," said Kelroy.

"Mine's apple and black currant," said William, gulping half of his glass in one mouthful.

Ainsley suddenly felt exhausted. It seemed so long ago that she and Harlan had been walking along the Fruitfly Bay shore, wondering how they could get an also-mom for their dad. Could it really have been only that morning that she had caught the dandelion and made the Kazillion Wish? She felt as though the day had gone on and on and on.

It was as though Harlan were reading her mind.

He said, "This is the most amazing day we've ever had. But I'm so tired I could fall asleep right here under the stars."

Yet even as he spoke, Harlan felt his left foot start to move. Soon, his toe started tapping on the grass, and then his leg began to twist at the knee, picking up the beat of William's theme music.

"Hey!" said Harlan. "What's going on?"

Next, his right foot joined in, shuffling up and down so that he had trouble keeping his balance. "Hey! Hey, my feet!"

Harlan glanced at his sister and couldn't help but smile. Ainsley was dancing wildly, but only from the waist down. Her arms were waving around, trying to keep balanced. She looked as astonished as he did.

Larry and Kelroy were also dancing crazily, four arms, five legs, and accompanying tentacles whizzing in all directions, and Zucchini was doing the most bizarre series of moves Harlan had ever seen. Bikini was grooving to the music while William was pulling the kind of funky moves that only a superhero would attempt.

"This one I call the Sputnik!" William yelled over the music, moonwalking before striking a pose and flicking his neck and arms, then twisting his hips theatrically and dancing off across the lawn.

"Wow, he can really move!" said Ainsley, giving in to the groove and dancing happily on the grass.

Harlan was still fighting it, but his hips were swaying, his feet moving, and his shoulders starting to twist to the music. "What's going on?" he yelled.

Zucchini and Bikini danced past, arms around each other, doing the Bow Foxtrot. "Lightning Juice," said Zucchini. "Tastes like fruit. Makes you dance in your pants!"

"Go with the flow, Joe," said William, as he danced past, doing a rumba with Ainsley.

"I haven't danced like this since I whacked my toe with a Martian hammer," cried Larry, dancing a difficult two-Martian conga chain with Kelroy. "And Martian hammers are bigger than Martian ducks."

"That's just another interesting fact about Martians," sang Kelroy.

Harlan finally gave in and danced like he had never danced before. They all jumped and leaped and boogied and swayed and grooved and got down to William's music, which seamlessly churned out a collection of pop favorites, from Kylie Minogue to Madonna. Harlan and Ainsley recognized a few of the songs, but with Lightning Juice in their bodies, they danced like crazy, no matter what was playing . . . that is until William's music began a country-and-western number and everybody stopped dead, the spell completely broken.

"Ah well, it was fun while it lasted!" said Bikini.

"Dancing is the only thing I like more than being a superhero!" declared William. "That was great."

Once they got their breath back, exhaustion set in for good. Harlan and Ainsley both had showers in the Bow bathroom, then came out for a delicious Bow meal.

"What are we having?" asked Harlan.

"Honey," said Bikini.

"Runny honey," added Zucchini.

"Yummy runny honey," said Bikini.

"Yummy runny honey made by our mommy," said Zucchini.

"Yummy runny honey made by our mommy on a day when it was sunny," said his sister.

"And the yummy runny honey made by our mommy on a day when it was sunny eventually comes out your bummy," shrieked Zucchini.

Everybody stared at one another.

"Pretty funny," said Larry.

"Kind of crummy," said Kelroy.

The Bows finally stopped rhyming long enough for everybody to eat dinner. And they finished the meal with mouthwatering cloud chocolate. Then they brushed their teeth, Larry and Kelroy went down the hall, and they all curled up in Bow beds, more ready than they'd ever been for sleep.

Until Ainsley sat bolt upright. "Harlan! What about Dad? We've been gone for hours and hours. He'll be worried sick."

"This has all been so amazing that I completely forgot about Fruitfly Bay!" Harlan said. "What are we going to do?"

"Leave it to me," said Bikini. "Hey, Zucchini?"

The Bow replied with a loud, whistling snore.

"Zucchini?" said Bikini.

Another big snore from Zucchini.

"ZUCCHINI SPACESTATION!" shrieked his sister.

"Hello! It's me! It is I! I am me! Ummm . . . why am I awake?" Zucchini launched himself out of bed.

"The children's father. He'll be worried," said Bikini.

"Hey, you're right, but I can fix it in a jiffy," said Zucchini. He reached into his bottomless coat pocket and grabbed his cell phone. "Hello? Zootfrog? . . . Oops . . . I forgot to dial. . . . Hello, Zootfrog? It's me, Zucchini. . . . yes, zee quest is verrrrrrry nice, thank you for asking. Everything is fantastic! There's just one more small thing. . . . Zee kids' father . . . Oh, you have? . . . Already? . . . Hey, zat's spectacularly, brilliantly, um, good. . . . Thanks a lot. . . . OK, you, too . . . I'll tell them. . . . Thanks again. . . . No, I don't know zee recipe for Dog Poo Porridge. . . . OK, see you."

He hung up. "Boy, those frongles eat some weird stuff. . . . Well, good night, everybody." He climbed back into bed and fell asleep in a second.

Harlan and Ainsley looked at each other, eyes wide. Harlan said very softly, "Zucchini? Zucchini? . . ."

There were snores from Zucchini until Bikini shrieked, "ZUCCHINI SPACESTATION!"

Zucchini leaped out of bed, eyes bulging. "It's great to be here. Thanks for having me. You've been a wonderful audience. I'll be here all week. Try zee beef."

"Zucchini, what did Zootfrog say about Dad?"

"Oh," he said, shrugging. "Relax, Harlan. He's not even worried."

"What do you mean he's not worried? Why isn't he worried?" asked Ainsley.

Zucchini yawned. "Because zee frongles have knocked him out."

"*What?*" yelled Harlan.

Two rooms away, Larry said to Kelroy, "There's a lot of yelling going on tonight."

"We Martians need our beauty sleep," said Kelroy.

"I'm tempted to sleep with my head in the ground," said Larry.

"That's a great idea, but you wouldn't be able to breathe."

"I hadn't thought of that. Oh well, good night."

"Good night."

Meanwhile, back in Zucchini's room, Harlan repeated his question. "The frongles did what?"

"They knocked your father out. Standard quest procedure." Zucchini shrugged. "You see, a Kazillion Wish quest might take anywhere from two days to several weeks, so if humans are involved, zee frongles have to make sure they have time. Zootfrog put a frongle fog spell on your father so he'll sleep peacefully until you two get back."

"But what if somebody comes over to the house? What if he gets a call from work? What if the lawn needs mowing?"

"Relax. You've never seen a frongle fog in action. Anyway, if worse comes to worst, Macklin can juggle his levers and work out any time issues."

"So, Dad's OK," said Ainsley.

"And we can take as long as we need to complete our quest," said Harlan.

"Which means we can relax and go to sleep."

"Hooray!" said Harlan. "Good night, Ainsley. Today has been amazing."

"Astonishing," agreed his sister.

"Today has been about five minutes too long," grumbled Zucchini. "How much did you miss me, Bikini, my sister?"

"Like an elephant would miss its trunk," Bikini murmured from her bed. "You?"

"Like Earth would miss zee moon."

And they all fell into a deep, deep sleep.

10

The Lord of Bark

The next morning was bright and sunny, not a hint of darkness anywhere. In fact, it was so sunny that they decided to have yummy runny honey made by Zucchini's mommy, which eventually would . . . actually, let's not start that again.

At last, they were ready to continue their quest, although there was one small thing.

"William," said Ainsley. "It's been great to meet you, and the way you scared off the darkness was awesome, but there's one more thing we need from you, I'm afraid. . . ."

"There is?" asked William. His puzzled expression clashed with his superhero outfit, complete with black shirt, gold sash, golden cape, and boots. Not to mention superhero theme music bubbling away in the background.

"Do you have something for us?"

"You want Lightning Juice? At this hour of the morning?"

"No, for our quest!"

"Our word! We need our word!" Harlan reminded him.

"The word! Of course," said William. "I'll give it to you now. Are you ready?"

Zucchini was already digging through his bottomless pocket to find his notebook. A baseball fell out. Then a football. An umbrella. A mango. A pineapple. A wand. A spare tire ("I don't know why I'm carrying that around!" he said). Five pieces of bubble wrap. A golf club. Finally, he found it.

"Ready," he yelled at last.

"OK, my word is 'birds,'" said William.

"Birds?" said Ainsley.

"Birds?" said Harlan.

"He said 'birds,'" said Larry helpfully.

"I heard it, too. Birds," agreed Kelroy.

"We Martians have fantastic hearing," said Larry.

"That's just another interesting . . ." began Kelroy.

"DON'T SAY IT!" shrieked Zucchini.

"Birds," confirmed William.

Zucchini was bouncing up and down on the spot. "Words. Birds. Girds. Wonka Nerds. Undeterred. Let me be heard. Soup must be stirred."

"Thanks, Zucchini. We've got it," said William. "Just write it down, please."

"OK," he said, scribbling furiously. "It. Zere you go. I wrote 'it' down."

"I'm so not buying into this," said William, shaking his head.

Bikini giggled helplessly. "Great joke, Bro."

"So our words so far read: 'Here's the thing birds,'" said Ainsley. "This makes less sense with every new addition."

"Stick with it, guys. The frongles know what they're doing," said William. "You're more than halfway there — only three challenges to go. But be careful. There are some dangerous and difficult times ahead."

"There are? Can you come with us?" asked Ainsley. "It would make me feel a lot better knowing there was a superhero alongside me."

"Sorry, Ainsley. This is your quest, not mine. And anyway, I have to keep an eye on that pesky darkness. I just got word that a couple of four-wheel drivers decided to go exploring and are driving headlong into the darkness as I speak. I'd better go and rescue them. Plus, my super-senses are picking up stirrings."

"What kind of stirrings?" asked Ainsley.

"I'm not sure yet, but something is afoot. I think it's out to the east, near the coast."

Harlan shook hands with the caped hero. "We're going to miss you, William . . . I mean, Lightning Rod."

"I have a feeling we'll meet again," he replied with a wink. "Good luck with the Lord of Bark." His theme music swelled from quiet background to stirring departure, and his entire body started to glow. He rose slowly into the air until he was floating above their heads. Then, with a wave and one final drumroll, he shot into the sky and flew away toward the darkness, as fast as a shooting star.

"Cool guy," said Larry.

"Bad fashion sense," said Kelroy.

"Here's the thing birds," said Ainsley, frowning.

"Those frongles love their crrrazy word games. But they're no good at rhymes," said Bikini.

"Let's find the next word," said Harlan. "I think it's going to be tricky."

"It is?" said Ainsley. "We don't know anything about this Lord of Bark. I mean, what bark? What sort of bark? Lord of what?"

"You won't like him. Note the wording of the poem," said Larry.

> **"'You must meet the one**
> **Who scares the dark,**
> **And demand a word**
> **From the Lord of Bark.'"**

"It sounds like there's going to be some *demanding*," said Ainsley.

"That's not the same as *asking*. Or *requesting*," agreed Kelroy. "*Demanding* means the Lord of Bark doesn't want to help."

Harlan and Ainsley shuffled their feet nervously, but Zucchini just shrugged.

"Well, zis is a Kazillion Wish quest, remember? It's

not all going to be smooth sailing, as it has been so far," he said.

"Smooth sailing? We've almost been eaten by a Chocolion, fallen off the biggest cliff in the world, risked our necks in an alien spacecraft — no offense, Larry and Kelroy — and survived Lightning Juice!" Harlan said.

"Yeah, nothing but fun, right, kids?" Zucchini beamed. "And now zee Lord of Bark awaits. Let's ride."

They all piled into *The Beast*, except for Bikini, who planned to do some shopping. "I'm fresh out of diamonds," she explained.

"What do you need diamonds for?" asked Ainsley.

"How else am I going to power up my Bow vacuum cleaner?"

Ainsley was sorry she'd asked.

Kelroy inserted the flower-shaped key into *The Beast*'s ignition.

The engine went *rrrr, rrrrr, rrrrr, rrrrr, rrrrr*.

Larry said, "Uh-oh . . . Umm, Kelroy, there's just one thing. . . ."

Everybody waited while he went to the bathroom, then got back in the front passenger seat.

The engine went *rrrr, rrrrr, rrrrr, rrrrr, rrrrr*.

Kelroy said, "Excuse me, just for a moment." And disappeared into Bikini's cottage.

He finally returned and reached for the flower-shaped key once more.

The engine went *rrrr, rrrrr, rrrrr, rrrrr, rrrrr*.

Kelroy said, "I think we're out of gas."

Larry said, "Try once more."

Kaboommmmmmmm! The Beast made a sound like a watermelon hitting a waterslide, and they took off, searing into the sky so fast that Ainsley's and Harlan's eyes watered and their tongues were glued to the roofs of their mouths.

"Mmm, mmm, mmmm grrnnn, hmmm, nmmnmm," said Harlan, which translated meant: "Spacecraft travel doesn't get any easier, does it?"

From under a huge pile of pillows, cushions, a full-size mattress, and three suits of armor, Zucchini replied, "Gmmm, jmmm, lmm, brmmm," which meant: "Oh, I don't know, I'm starting to enjoy it."

Just then, the spacecraft reached the high point of its journey, slowed, stopped, hovered in the air, and then plummeted back toward Earth.

"Aaaaaaaaaaaaaaaaaaarrrrrggggghhhhh!" screamed Harlan and Ainsley.

"Bgggggrrrrrrrrrppmmmmmmmmmmmmmmmmmmmmm!" screamed Zucchini.

The Beast hurtled toward an enormous paddock that had incredibly green grass and one ginormous tree right in the middle. Next to it was a small hut in the middle of the paddock. *The Beast* was heading right for it.

"Kelroy, the hut!" screamed Ainsley.

"We're going to crash!" screeched Harlan.

"Wheeeeeeeeeee!" squealed Larry.

The Beast hurtled at the hut until there was only a matter of feet till impact — the spacecraft was traveling at 1,000 miles per hour (read: fast!).

Then, nanoseconds before they would have

slammed straight through the hut's wooden roof, Kelroy calmly braked, and the spacecraft screeched to a halt, with less than 10 inches to spare.

Kelroy whistled as he edged a few feet to the left and set *The Beast* down neatly on the grass. The small bobble-head dog on the dashboard nodded its head happily.

In the back, Ainsley's, Harlan's, and Zucchini's hearts slowly realized it was OK to beat again.

"Excellent driving, Kelroy," said Larry.

"Thanks. I think I could have waited a little before I braked, but never mind."

"Waited a little?" cried Zucchini. "Waited a LITTLE? We missed it by inches. Crazy Martians!"

Everybody clambered out on wobbly legs and looked at the hut. A sign above the door read: LORD OF BARK SOUVENIR STAND.

Ainsley opened the door and her eyes goggled. There, standing behind the counter, was her teacher, Ms. Grassmuncher. The Lawnmower. The one who spoke so slowly that she drove her class crazy.

"Hello . . . ," she said, before a long pause. ". . . Can . . . I . . . (pause) . . . (another pause) . . . help . . . (an unfeasibly long pause) . . . you?"

"Ms. Grassmuncher!" exclaimed Ainsley.

"How . . . do . . . (pause) . . . you know . . . (big pause) . . . my name?" she asked eventually.

"You're my teacher! It's me, Ainsley Banana!"

Ms. Grassmuncher stared at Ainsley for so long that they thought she'd frozen. Finally, she said . . . (after another excruciatingly long pause) . . . ,"No."

"No?" asked Ainsley, totally confused. "No, what?"

"That's . . . (pause) . . . my . . . (very long pause) . . . sister, Gristle."

"Ms. Grassmuncher's first name is Gristle?" Ainsley started to laugh.

"So . . . you think . . . (long pause) . . . that's funny . . . (very, very long pause) . . . huh?"

"Um, no."

Just then, the back door opened and Harlan did a double take as his teacher, Alfred Stranglenose, walked in, stooping because he was far too tall for the tiny hut.

"So, we have visitors, no?" he boomed in his loud voice.

"Er, yes," said Harlan. "Hello, Mr. Stranglenose, sir."

"I don't know you, do I? Yes?" said Mr. Stranglenose.

"Yes, I'm in your class . . . Harlan Banana."

"I don't think I have a class, do I, yes?"

Harlan blinked in confusion.

"I think that might be my brother, Alfred, wouldn't it be, no? Yes?"

"Umm," said Harlan. "You're Alfred Stranglenose's brother?"

"I am Arthur Stranglenose, no? That's who you're addressing, yes?"

Harlan and Ainsley gave each other a look.

"You speak like an idiot, yes?" said Zucchini, who had walked in behind Harlan and Ainsley.

"That's not very polite, is it, yes? You ought to watch your mouth, no?" said Mr. Stranglenose.

Ms. Grassmuncher was also saying something but

the pause was so long that nobody waited around for whatever she was planning to say.

"Yes? No? Maybe? Yes?" said Zucchini, bouncing up and down on the spot. "You're driving me crazy!"

"Watch yourself, Bow, yes?" said Mr. Stranglenose.

"Yes, bess, guess, less, tess, confess, countess, west . . . best, lest, nest, messed . . . ," rambled Zucchini.

"Do you and Ms. Grassmuncher own this souvenir shop?" Harlan asked.

"That would be right if it were correct, I do believe, no?" said Stranglenose. "We met at a school social night, I do believe, isn't that right, yes?"

Ms. Grassmuncher opened her mouth. . . . There was a very long pause. . . .

"Do you work for zee Lord of Bark?" asked Zucchini, who wasn't about to wait for Ms. Grassmuncher to finally say something.

"Yes, we do, don't we . . . no?" Mr. Stranglenose said. "We're in charge of merchandise, yes?"

Harlan, Ainsley, and Zucchini looked around the shop for the first time. There were rows and rows of shelves and display stands. All completely empty.

"Do you have any souvenirs that might tell us something about the Lord of Bark?" said Ainsley.

"I'm afraid . . . ," said Ms. Grassmuncher, before a long, long pause.

The pause continued.

After which there was a pause.

Harlan, Ainsley, and Zucchini exchanged glances.

"You're afraid? You're afraid of what?" Zucchini

finally exploded. "Spiders? Ghosts? Goblins? Grass? Fleas? Clouds? Cars? Chocolate? Gold? Cats? Jelly? Chimneys? Widths? Sneezing? Sand? Flowers? BATS!"

"Afraid . . . we're fresh . . . (pause) . . . out of . . . (long pause) . . . (and yet another long pause) . . . souvenirs," Ms. Grassmuncher finally managed.

"OK, we're out of here. This is a silly place," said Zucchini. "Let's go meet Bark boy."

"I wouldn't advise that, would I, yes?" said Stranglenose.

"Why not?" asked Harlan.

"The Lord of Bark doesn't like visitors, does he, no? You'll be sorry, yes?"

Harlan and Ainsley stared at him. Ms. Grassmuncher's mouth was open again.

There was a horribly long pause. Then a gap and another pause.

Ms. Grassmuncher finally said, "Suckers!"

Harlan, Ainsley, and Zucchini left the shop.

Larry and Kelroy were decked out, head to toe, in baseball caps, T-shirts, streamers, scarves, and flags, all emblazoned with the words: I LUV BARK.

"Where did you get those?" asked Harlan.

"A cardboard box behind the hut," explained Kelroy.

"We went exploring. Martians like exploring," said Larry.

"That's just another interesting fact about . . ." said Kelroy.

"Yes, yes, yes," said Zucchini. "I think it's time we found zis Lord guy."

But where? Apart from the hut, all they could see as far as the horizon were flat, grassy fields. Except for an absolutely enormous tree, about a mile away. It was so huge that it could have been a skyscraper, reaching so far into the sky that they could barely make out the branches at the top. It was by far the biggest tree Harlan and Ainsley had ever laid eyes on. It might have been an oak tree but the leaves were so high in the sky that it was difficult to tell.

"Boy, zat's some tree, huh?" said Zucchini, a little unnecessarily.

"Big," agreed Larry.

"Lots of bark," said Kelroy.

"Of course!" said Harlan.

"Bark!" yelled Ainsley. "The Lord of Bark! The Lord of Bark is a giant tree!"

"Maybe it's like the Great Deku Tree in *Zelda*, where the tree talks," said Harlan.

"Or maybe it's like the *Magic Faraway Tree*, where the Lord lives in a room at the very top, like Moonface," suggested Ainsley.

"Or maybe it's just a tree," said Larry.

"Let's find out," said Kelroy.

They headed toward it, with Larry and Kelroy laboring under their souvenir clothing flags. Luckily, they each had five legs to make walking easier.

It took about thirty-five minutes to reach the base of the tree. Up close, the trunk was so thick that it was like staring at a wall. The trunk was so large that it was as though they were standing next to a huge, round tower, with the bark stretching 150 feet in each direction before disappearing around the curve.

They looked up. The lower branches waved gently, covered in leaves, 1,500 feet above them.

"Going to be tricky to climb!" said Zucchini.

"If only William were here to fly us," said Harlan.

"We can't be expected to climb." Ainsley was frowning. "Anyway, I'm not sure that the Lord of Bark would be very happy if we tried to climb all over him."

She took five or six steps backward and stood very straight. "Hello, Lord of Bark."

Nothing.

Larry and Kelroy sniggered a little. "Try it again."

"Why not say, 'Take me to your leader'?" suggested Kelroy.

Ainsley shrugged. She addressed the massive tree again. "Take me to your leader!"

Larry and Kelroy giggled helplessly. "I've always wanted to hear somebody say that," Larry said.

"Big joke among aliens," Kelroy explained.

"You two aren't helping," Harlan glared. "Zucchini, what's around the back of the tree?"

Zucchini was wandering around the corner. "Oh, nothing, I don't think. I'd say it's just more . . ."

And then he was hit right on the head by a large rock, and he fell down, unconscious.

"Hey!" shouted Ainsley. "Zucchini!"

"The rock came from behind the tree!" yelled Harlan.

He charged around the corner, arms up to protect his head, but found nothing.

Ainsley patted the Bow's face. "Zucchini?" she said. "Zucchini Spacestation!" He snored gently.

"Whoever it was must have sneaked farther around the trunk," said Harlan, pointing to the left. "Larry, Kelroy, you go that way and I'll go this way. We'll cut them off."

"Who, us?" said Larry, looking startled.

Kelroy glanced at Zucchini, still out cold. "We Martians aren't supposed to get in rock fights."

Larry looked shifty. "It's bad for, umm, our complexion."

"I thought you Martians didn't get scared," said Harlan, arms folded.

"Oh, we're not scared!" said Larry.

"Not even a bit scared," agreed Kelroy.

"Let's clear that up right now. . . . We're totally, utterly unconcerned about the idea that a giant rock might knock us out the moment we walk around the back of that tree," Larry added.

"It hadn't even occurred to us," said Kelroy.

"It's not as though our hearts are leaping at the prospect that there could be some kind of monster lurking around there," Larry said.

Kelroy even attempted a laugh. "Ha-ha-ha-ha-ha." It came out pretty weakly, even for a robotic Martian voice.

"Larry and Kelroy, we really need your help," said Ainsley.

Harlan nodded. "Just make a lot of noise as you

walk. You'll scare whoever it is away, and they'll bump into me."

Larry and Kelroy looked at each other. "Good plan!" said Larry.

Producing specially branded Lord of Bark trumpets from among their merchandise, they started honking loudly and walking around the trunk to the right.

Harlan took a deep breath. He could hear the Martians' trumpets blaring on the other side of the massive trunk. It sounded as though one of the Martians was trying to play a Muppets song.

Harlan crept to the left, expecting another large rock to come flying at him at any second. All he could hear was the Martians' souvenir trumpets honking wildly. *Honk! Blart! Honk! Honk! Hoot!* Suddenly, there were two big thuds. And silence.

"Uh-oh," said Harlan.

He sprinted around the massive trunk until he found Larry and Kelroy, out cold, with large rocks next to their heads — their trumpets still in their hands.

Harlan was terrified. "Ainsley?" he yelled. He began to panic.

He raced back around the massive trunk and found Ainsley with Zucchini, who was snuggled up to a teddy bear, snoring quietly.

"What happened?" asked Ainsley.

"Larry and Kelroy have been knocked out, too," Harlan said. "It's just you and me. We need a plan."

He put his index fingers to his temples and scrunched up his face. "OK, so far, there have been three big rocks. There's three hundred sixty degrees of the tree that we have to cover and we can only see twenty-five percent of the tree at any one time. That means the enemy could be anywhere in the other seventy-five percent, but if we cover fifty percent each . . ."

Ainsley shrugged. *"For Dad!"* she yelled, and charged off around the tree, screaming a war cry.

Harlan shook his head at his sister's fearlessness, and said softly, "Yeah, OK, that was Plan B. For Dad!"

He headed off around the massive tree trunk again, ready to face whatever had knocked out his three companions. His imagination was going crazy, conjuring up all sorts of rock-throwing giants. It occurred to him that this could be the end. His quest finished, along with his life. Harlan gulped.

Suddenly, he was struck, smack on the head, right near the temple, by . . . a tiny pebble.

"Ouch!" he cried. And then he started laughing.

Harlan was facing a tiny dog, so small that it only came up to his knees. It was fluffy and white with a couple of brown patches on its back. When he didn't fall down, it started yapping furiously. The dog stood up on its hind legs with another tiny pebble in one paw. It hurled the pebble, and Harlan caught it easily.

"Woof! Nice catch," panted the dog.

"Thanks," said Harlan.

They stared at each other.

"Arufff! I've run out of big rocks," the dog explained.

"Lucky for me," said Harlan. "You can't be the one who knocked out my friends!"

"Grrrr, woof! I'm afraid so. Don't let my size fool you."

"Why?"

"Ruff! Because I am Lord of this domain," said the little dog. "I refuse to let trespassers into my kingdom!"

"Lord?" Harlan repeated. "You mean, you? You're the Lord of Bark?"

"Woof! Of course I am. And don't sound so surprised. What did you think? That some old tree was the Lord of Bark?"

"Er . . . maybe." Harlan stood tall. "My name is Harlan Banana, and I am on a frongle-sent noble quest with my sister, Ainsley. I demand that you give us the word we need to continue our quest."

"Growwwwwllll! Sorry, kid. No can do. Frongles, schmongles."

"Listen, the Bow and the Martians are my friends. You knocked them out cold. I'm not in a good mood. Hand over the word!"

"Ruff! I'll hand over this," said the dog, suddenly producing one more big rock from behind the tree. He hurled it at Harlan, who ducked so quickly that he fell flat on his back. By the time he regained his feet, the Lord of Bark was scampering across the field toward a small skateboard. The dog jumped onto it and flames licked out from underneath as he soared into the sky.

The flying board banked in a steep curve and came straight for Harlan. In that moment, the sky darkened and thunder crashed all around. The little dog's eyes burned like evil lasers as he charged, teeth bared and growling ominously. Suddenly, he didn't look like such a harmless little dog. Harlan had to dive for safety, and lay cowering on the ground with his hands over his head until the Lord of Bark had swooped past and shot into the sky.

Even through his torn T-shirt, Harlan's back felt singed by the flames of the skateboard. He lifted his head as the dog zoomed away with a very evil doggy laugh. "Woof! Woof! Woof! Ha-ha-ha-ha-ha!"

"Bad dog! Bad dog!" Harlan yelled.

Harlan stared at the disappearing animal as Ainsley came running around the corner.

"Harlan, are you OK?"

"Yeah, I'm fine, but . . ."

"But what?" Ainsley noticed tears welling in her brother's eyes.

"The Lord of Bark . . . he was a small dog," Harlan said. "He escaped."

"What? A small dog?" repeated Ainsley. "Are you OK, Harlan?"

"Yes, but that's not the point. You don't get it. . . . I didn't get our word. He refused to give it to me."

They stared at each other. "Oh no," said Ainsley at last.

Back by the tree, they found their companions sitting up, rubbing their heads. The Martians' antennae were glowing in several different colors and their tentacles were waving wildly as they regained their senses. Zucchini's head was surrounded by small birds, tweeting.

"I thought that only happened in cartoons," murmured Harlan.

"Did anybody get the number of zat bus?" asked the Bow.

"My head feels like a Plutonian's," said Larry.

"Is that bad?" asked Ainsley.

"Very bad, Ainsley Banana. Definitely very bad," said Kelroy.

After a few minutes, Zucchini and the Martians had recovered enough to listen to Harlan's story. Zucchini bounced up and down on the spot for quite a few minutes. Eventually, it occurred to Ainsley and Harlan that he was doing something they hadn't seen him attempt before — he was thinking.

"I've got it!" Zucchini said suddenly.

"You have?" asked Harlan, hopefully.

"Well, not 'it.' I haven't got 'it,' if what you think of as 'it' is some kind of solution to zee fact that you missed getting the word from zee Lord of Bark. That 'it,' I'm afraid, I can't help you with at this exact moment."

"Then what have you got?" asked Ainsley.

"I've got an idea."

"Which is?"

"A secret."

"A secret!" Harlan exploded. "Why is it a secret?"

The Bow gave them a sly smile. "Because secrets are fun!"

"OK, Zucchini, why don't you tell me the secret?" said Ainsley. "Secrets are even more fun if you share them with just one person."

"Actually, you might be right. It is fun to share a secret. . . . But only you, Ainsley," Zucchini said. He whispered into her ear, "I was thinking of phoning Zootfrog to see what she thought we should do."

"Phone Zootfrog!" said Ainsley loudly. "That's a great idea!"

"Hey, zat was a secret!" complained Zucchini. "But, you agree? You think it's a good idea?"

"Definitely. Maybe there's a replacement challenge we can attempt," said Harlan.

"I hope it's chess," said Larry, still holding his head.

"Or knitting. Anything without rocks," agreed Kelroy.

Zucchini dialed Zootfrog's number on his cell phone. He listened for a long time and then said, "Zootfrog? Hi, it's me, Zucchini Spacestation! Yes, well, thanks. Fine . . . Great . . . There's been a bit of a hiccup in zee Kazillion Wish quest. . . . We need to talk. . . . We'll come to you, then. . . . What was zat? . . . Right-o . . . Bye!"

He hung up.

"What did she say?" asked Harlan.

"She wasn't there. I got her answering machine."

Ainsley said, "But you had an entire conversation!"

"Frongle answering machines are a little different from human ones, you know. Zee machine said to come back to Fruitfly Bay, pronto. Big things are happening there."

Larry and Kelroy exchanged a lightning-quick look. Harlan saw it.

"Big things?" asked Harlan. "What kind of big things?"

"It wouldn't say. . . . It agrees with me. . . . Secrets are fun," Zucchini said.

There was no time to lose. The travelers left the giant tree and made their way back to *The Beast*. Ainsley detoured long enough to poke her head inside the souvenir hut, but it was empty. Ms. Grassmuncher and Mr. Stranglenose were nowhere to be seen.

The Beast took a couple of tries but then, with a sound like a giant apple thudding into a rubber swimming pool, it blasted into space, soared into the stratosphere, tilted on an angle, and plunged toward home. Martian driving permitting, they were on their way back to Fruitfly Bay.

11

Swimming with Sharks

The Beast touched down outside Harlan and Ainsley's house — if you can call screaming headlong at the Earth right up until the last second when you somehow screech to a halt "touching down." The spacecraft had barely stopped smoking before the children were flying through the front door, yelling for their father.

They thundered upstairs to their father's bedroom. Suddenly, they stopped. Spencer Banana was curled up in bed, wearing his pajamas, snoring softly. Harlan and Ainsley crept out of the room.

"The frongle fog! We haven't completed our quest yet. We should let him sleep until we're done," said Harlan.

"He looks so peaceful," Ainsley said.

They took the opportunity to change their clothes before heading back outside. Zucchini had just managed to remove the last of his protective gear while Larry and Kelroy were playing Martian hacky sack soccer, using six hacky sacks, all ten of their feet, and their eight tentacles.

Next, Harlan and Ainsley raced around the corner to their mom's house. The door was open. They tiptoed inside and found her fast asleep as well.

"She looks even more peaceful than Dad," said Harlan.

They looked at their mother for a long time, until Ainsley said very quietly, "I wish they were asleep together."

"You know what? . . . I don't," said Harlan.

His sister stared at him in amazement. "Really?"

"You're younger. You don't remember how they used to fight, how they made each other grumpy, how they even made each other cry. I think they're better apart. We still get to see both of them, but they don't yell at each other all the time. I never thought I'd say this, but I think they're happier now."

"Except for Dad being lonely, listening to that sad music, and hugging us like he's afraid to let go."

"Yeah, except for that."

Their mother stirred in bed and turned over. Ainsley whispered, "Let's go. We don't want to wake her up."

Outside, Martian hacky sack was in full flight, and a certain Bow was making enthusiastic, if hopelessly unsuccessful, attempts to join in. When they saw the children, the Martians put down their sacks.

"Let's get to the beach," said Larry, looking very serious.

They hurried past the snack bar and the bakery, then the school.

"Harlan?" said Ainsley nervously.

"I know. I've noticed it, too . . . or, more to the point, not noticed it."

"Noticed what?" asked Kelroy.

"Not noticed what?" asked Larry.

"Noticed zat we should not be noticing zat which isn't what?" asked Zucchini.

"The entire town . . . it's deserted," Harlan said.

And he was right. Fruitfly Bay was a ghost town. No matter where they looked — down every street, in the school, and in the shops — the place was completely empty.

"Where is everyone?" asked Harlan.

"Look, there's Zootfrog," said Ainsley. "Let's ask her."

Sure enough, the golden frongle who had set them on their Kazillion Wish quest was sitting on a swing on the shore, near the beach where they had first met. Zootfrog looked grave as they approached.

"Hello, Bananas," she said. "Your quest has been going well. The Chocolion didn't eat you. Martian space travel hasn't killed you. You even escaped the Zone of Darkness. Well done."

"But the Lord of Bark got away, Zootfrog. I *demanded* a word, like the poem said I should, but he attacked me and escaped," Harlan said.

Zootfrog gave him a long look, as though making up her mind. Then she sighed. "Well, you may have a chance to get that word sooner than you think, Harlan.

Or it may not matter anymore. There are bigger things going on."

"Bigger zan a noble Kazillion Wish quest?" asked Zucchini.

"Yes," Zootfrog said. "Normally, we could not even imagine discussing such matters in front of humans, but Harlan and Ainsley are so far into their quest that they deserve to be part of this. Assuming you want to. . . The next few hours could be extremely dangerous. You might have noticed that the entire town is under a frongle fog. If you'd rather be asleep and forget everything that's happened, I would understand."

"No way," said Ainsley immediately.

"Not a chance," agreed Harlan. "We haven't finished our quest yet, and we're not stopping until we do. Besides, what could be more dangerous than hanging out with Zucchini, Larry, and Kelroy?"

"Good point," said the frongle. "OK, then you're in. It's time to visit our friends who cut the foam."

"Our friends who cut the foam!" Ainsley exclaimed. "They're in the Kazillion Wish poem! Cool."

"Yes. And the foam is the surf," said Zootfrog. "Let's go!"

At the water's edge, Zucchini reached into his bottomless coat pocket and pulled out a complete scuba diving suit, with an air tank, a mask, and flippers. As he struggled into the wet suit, Zootfrog produced two pairs of sunglasses, each with a small tube coming off the frame.

"Your scuba gear . . . standard frongle issue," she said,

handing them to Harlan and Ainsley. "You'll be able to see and breathe underwater. No need to worry about running out of air. Just breathe normally and you'll be fine," Zootfrog said.

"Amazing," said Ainsley.

"Zucchini, you don't have any more fins in your pocket, do you?" asked Harlan.

"Why, sure!" said the Bow, producing seven or eight pairs. "What size do you need?"

Soon they were all suited up, and Zootfrog led the way into the surf. The kids dived under the waves, then resurfaced, swimming along the top of the water, until they realized everybody else had stayed underwater. Harlan and Ainsley gave each other a glance, Ainsley shrugged, they checked that their frongle scuba goggles were in place, and then ducked below the waves.

Harlan could breathe as naturally as he had back on the beach. Ainsley gave him a thumbs-up.

"This is so cool!" she said, and then smiled as she realized she could talk underwater as well. "C'mon, you two." Zootfrog shot ahead like a golden fish. "There's not much time." Harlan and Ainsley swam faster, following the thrashing legs, tentacles, and arms of Zucchini, Zootfrog, and the Martians.

"'You must help our friends / Who cut the foam,'" Ainsley said. "We're still on our quest."

"Yes, except that something big is going on, too," Harlan said. "Zootfrog looks worried."

Before long they reached a sheer rock wall. Zootfrog led the way through a narrow gap about one-third of the way up from the bottom, followed by Larry, Kelroy, and Zucchini. The children were last through the small opening. It led into an enormous cavern, lit by the sunlight filtering gently through the ocean from above. Massive rock walls enclosed the space, which was about three times as big as a football field. The entire cavern was filled with at least a thousand dolphins, all chattering madly. One dolphin, with a pure white stripe down its side, glided over to meet them.

"Zootfrog, thank you for coming. Zucchini, I haven't seen you for some time. Please, no Bow greetings! I'm getting too old for that."

Zucchini beamed. In Bow terms, being told your greeting was too frightening was a huge compliment.

"Thank you, King Dorsal, Your Highness. I would not dream of greeting you with anything other than a . . . 'Why, howdy.'"

The dolphin turned to Larry and Kelroy. "It is indeed an honor to have such fine Martians alongside us in this time of peril. Larry and Kelroy, you know that you are most welcome to stay for as long as you wish."

"Thanks, Chief," said Kelroy.

"We Martians like dolphins. They're our second favorite aquatic creatures," said Larry.

"That's just another interesting fact about Martians," said Kelroy.

The dolphin gazed at Harlan and Ainsley with a mixture of curiosity and fear.

"Humans, Zootfrog? It's very rare to see frongles or Bows accompanied by humans. I assume there is a good reason for this?" The dolphin turned to the children. "I'm sorry, I don't mean to be rude, but this is most unusual."

Zootfrog bowed low before the dolphin. "Your Excellency, of course there is a good reason. May I introduce Harlan and Ainsley Banana, residents of Fruitfly Bay and currently crusading on a noble quest, a Kazillion Wish quest, in fact. On their journey they have shown great courage in the face of the Chocolion and have demonstrated intelligence and an unwavering loyalty to their friends. I believe they will be an asset in what is to come, and I think we can trust them to keep dolphin secrets, just as they are now entrusted with frongle and Bow knowledge."

"High praise, indeed. I respect Zootfrog's judgment. I am pleased to meet you, Harlan and Ainsley Banana. As with the Martians, my water kingdom is yours to treat as your own home until this is over."

"With respect, Your Highness, sir, until *what* is over?" Harlan asked.

As if on cue, there was a murmur from the back of

the enormous cavern, and a chattering swept to the front like a wave. King Dorsal turned to one of his commanders. "What's happening?"

"Something is coming, Your Excellency. Something big."

"Is it them? We're not nearly ready."

"We don't know, Your Highness. We must wait."

The chattering swelled again. Harlan and Ainsley exchanged glances with Larry and Kelroy.

The dolphin king relaxed. "Phew . . . it's only the sharks."

Ainsley froze as the water above them filled with dark shapes. Hundreds, then thousands of sharks appeared. Enormous sharks, small sharks, hammerheads, sleek gray sharks, sharks with stripes.

She felt Zootfrog's tiny hand on her arm. "Relax, Ainsley, the sharks are our friends. They get a bum rap from humans, but most of the time they're peace-loving creatures."

"I thought that dolphins and sharks hated one another. I read that dolphins were capable of killing sharks by butting them with their hard noses," said Harlan.

"Just because we could, doesn't mean we do," said one of the king's assistants. "Most of the time, we stay out of one another's way and get on fine. Sometimes, like now, we work together."

King Dorsal went to greet the sharks, making a point of addressing an enormous whale shark at the head of the massive school. Harlan swam over to Zootfrog.

"What's going on?"

The frongle looked embarrassed. "Harlan, I'm sorry. You still haven't been briefed. The dolphins are under attack. So are the sharks and so are we."

"Under attack? Who from?"

Zootfrog looked as though she could barely say the name. "Fishface."

"Fishface," repeated Ainsley. "We keep hearing that name. Who is Fishface?"

"Not *who*, Ainsley, *what*. The fishface are a race of aggressive underwater beings. Most of the time, they live in the deepest reaches of the ocean, a long way from our friends who cut the foam. But every now and then, they decide to make a play for the surface. Legend has it that the fishface were land-dwellers once, and want to walk the earth again."

"What are they like?" asked Harlan.

"They're fierce and they're very strong; immensely strong. Our intelligence is that a massive fishface army is gathering a few miles away. They plan to attack us and take over Fruitfly Bay."

"Not scared, not scared, not scared," said Larry.

"We should call the police! Or the army!" said Harlan.

"No, this is frongle business," said Zootfrog. "Very few humans can know about it."

"But why?" Harlan said. "The human army would blitz a fishface army in a second."

"Maybe, maybe not," said Zootfrog. "But we must not reveal the frongle world, the Bow world, and all the other magical worlds to which you've been exposed, to other humans. We can't risk that. Anyway, the best way to beat the fishface is through good, old-fashioned magic . . . with a bit of a frongle surprise thrown in."

"Meaning?" asked Ainsley.

"You'll find out." Zootfrog grinned. "Wait here, I'll be right back."

Harlan and Ainsley floated around the cavern, smiling and nodding to dolphins. They were less comfortable with the sharks that occasionally drifted by, but Harlan, being Harlan, was fascinated by the way the sharks watched them with curious eyes, one on each side of their gray heads — did they see two images at once? Or did the images somehow link up? Or was there a huge gap in their vision, where their snout was? The only thing he was certain of was that they didn't smile much.

"Are you sure the sharks *are* friendly?" he asked Zucchini.

"As long as zey don't feel hungry or threatened. Then it's chompy, chompy, chomp," said the Bow.

"Thanks, Zucchini, I feel so much better."

Zootfrog was busy talking to the dolphin king and the giant whale shark. The ocean surface glistened far above.

Just then, a small human shape shot into the cavern, swimming faster than any figure Harlan and Ainsley had ever seen. The figure took a quick look around the cavern, spoke to a couple of the dolphins, and then spotted the dolphin king. The human was a girl, about ten years old, with shortish brown hair. She was wearing frongle scuba goggles, plus enormous flippers that powered her through the water.

"Zat's Georgina," explained Zucchini. "She's one gutsy kid. She's such a great swimmer and so brave that zee dolphins have asked her to help."

"I'm surprised you haven't met her, Banana people," said Larry, his tentacles swirling in the current.

"Why?" asked Ainsley.

"Your father and her mother go way back."

"Way back where?"

"Just way back." Harlan could have sworn Kelroy was smiling. "Ask her."

Georgina finished delivering her message to the dolphin king and whale shark, and swam over. "Hi, Zucchini, you crazy Bow." She looked at the Banana kids. "A Kazillion Wish quest, huh? I only know one other human who has ever managed it. You two must have seen amazing things and done some incredible stuff."

"Well, we've had our moments." Harlan stammered and blushed as Ainsley gave him a look.

They didn't have time to talk further because Zootfrog swam up. "OK, everybody. The latest word is that the fishface army is on the move, two miles away and closing fast."

Ainsley gulped. Harlan turned pale.

Larry squeezed his eyes shut and said, "Not even a little bit scared, not even a little bit scared, not even a little bit scared."

"Lucky we're already wet or I'd have to change my pants again." Zucchini blushed.

Harlan was thinking. "We'd better come up with a plan. Does anybody know anything about traditional defense positions in land-water battles?"

Georgina raised an eyebrow at him, offered one serious nod for luck, and kicked her flippers, powering off into the thick of the dolphin army. Harlan definitely wanted to get to know her better and he had lots of questions to ask her. Ainsley wanted to swim off and fight by her side.

But Zootfrog was approaching fast. "It's time to head back to Fruitfly Bay," she said. "The dolphins and sharks are ready to defend the ocean kingdom. We're in charge of the land. Let's go."

12

The Frighteningly Fierce
Fishface Fight

A couple of dolphins offered to take them back to shore. All they had to do was hold on to the dolphins' dorsal fins and not let go. Impending war or not, Harlan couldn't help but look at his sister with an enormous smile as they sped through the water, their hair flying in the watery wake.

She smiled right back. "I've spoken to cats and you've ridden a dolphin. Only one wish to go."

"Yeah, the big one. This is even better than I could have imagined. *Woo-hoo!*"

Far too quickly, they were at the shoreline. The tension was rising. The Banana kids sensed that events were moving faster than they could keep up with, and suddenly, their Kazillion Wish quest seemed trivial, compared to the alarming developments on the fishface front.

As they swam back to the surface, Harlan and Ainsley waved good-bye to their dolphin rides and a small blue shark, who had come along to ensure they were safe. The dolphins chattered briefly, and the shark waved a fin before flitting back into the deep.

Zootfrog led the way to the beach, and Harlan and Ainsley paused to take in the extraordinary sight.

An amazing collection of creatures was gathered by the seashore, looking serious and purposeful. Lightning Rod was there, shining in a golden light and accompanied, as ever, by his faithful theme music, playing a dramatic but definitely heroic tune. He was deep in conversation with his brother, Macklin, who was wearing pure white armor and carrying a remote control with tiny levers and gauges to move the stars.

The cats from the Starry Eye Café: Choo Choo, Co Co, and Rico were wearing cat armor — super-thick fur, stronger than steel.

"Do you think the fishface will smell?" asked Co Co.

"No more than you, smelly," replied Rico.

"Says you, birdbrain," Co Co said.

"Hey, we're about to save the world. Zip it!" said Choo Choo.

"He started it," sulked Rico.

"Did not," Co Co said.

"Peace and love, cats." Macklin sighed.

"What do you mean, 'peace and love'? The fishface are about to arrive! Crazy lever boy." The cats all had a chuckle.

"Crazy lever *cats*," said a fourth, familiar-looking cat.

"Scramble?" gasped Ainsley. Sure enough, it was their dad's cat, giving her a nod and a wink as he stayed close to Macklin's motley trio of cat warriors.

But as if that weren't enough, next to Scramble sat a tiny guinea pig, wearing spiky silver armor and a silver helmet with a giant blue feather. It was clutching a massive double-headed hammer that was at least twelve times his size.

"Log? Is that you? Mom's all-but-permanently-asleep guinea pig?" Ainsley said.

"I say: Fishface, end of the race!" Log squeaked. Harlan had to smile.

A few yards away, a huge squadron of frongles was assembled, dressed for battle. They looked exactly like Zootfrog, except that they were wearing bright orange armor. Next to them stood Zanzibar, Bikini, and at least sixty Bows.

Zucchini gave a yelp

of delight and bowed low. "I'd greet you all individually, but we have to save our bodies and our strength for battle against zee nasty, nasty, nasty bad old fishie-faces."

"You're right, Cousin," said Zanzibar. "Consider us greeted."

Larry and Kelroy whooped with excitement when a bunch of peculiar animals lumbered out from behind all the Bows and frongles. There was a giant pink ball of fluff, and a green one, both with ten legs, giant horns, twelve eyes, and antennae popping out of the top of their heads. The creatures made a strange humming noise that was occasionally broken up by a honk.

"Water Bucket Head! Vacuum Cleaner Brain!" Larry yelled.

Then a simply enormous duck and a tiny horse also emerged. "Quack Quack Bric-a-Brac! Jingle Bells Batman Smells!" cried Larry.

"Those fishie-faces won't be expecting serious Martian pet action." Zucchini grinned.

Suddenly, Ainsley and Harlan gave their own small cries of joy as they spotted a giant lion, its magnificent body shining in the sunlight and its rich mane framing its huge face. The lion looked intently at them through incredibly green eyes.

"Chocolion!" yelled Harlan.

"You're here!" shouted Ainsley, running over to give him her biggest hug.

"Hello, Banana children. I've been following your adventures with interest. Congratulations on getting so far. Let's see off the fishface so that you can complete your quest," said the Chocolion. "Then as soon as the battle is over, we can share some chocolate."

"Umm, chockie-puss, I think we'd better concentrate on surviving zee battle first," said Zucchini.

"I can hardly bring myself to say it, but Zucchini Spacestation might be right," said Zootfrog, looking toward the water.

Just then, a strange noise came from the beach. It sounded like water boiling but louder, as though something were bubbling under the surface of the ocean. Fierce flashes, like lightning, sizzled under the waves. Every now and then, a dolphin burst from the water, curved in the air, and dived back into the fray. Harlan felt a cold dread run down his spine.

"Get ready, everybody, the fishface are here. Grab a weapon," yelled Zootfrog, passing out shiny silver guns. They were huge, each with a big silver barrel about as wide as a tennis ball container, attached to a glass cylinder that glowed purple, orange, and green.

"What on earth are these?" Ainsley stared at her gun.

"The fishface are in for a surprise. These are frongle-blasters!"

Ainsley looked even more uncertain. "I'm not going to shoot anybody!"

"Yeah, we're pacifists," said Harlan.

"Eh, I like pace as much as zee next Bow — zee quicker, zee better — but these are desperate times," yelled Zucchini.

"Not pace . . . pacifist. Peace, not war," explained Harlan.

"Listen," Larry said with an unusually serious look on his Martian face. "Zucchini is right. These *are* desperate times. We don't like hurting anybody, either, but the frongle-blasters don't kill. The results of a direct hit are actually pretty funny."

"How can they be?" asked Ainsley.

"Trust me," said Larry, still earnest. "We Martians are forbidden by intergalactic law to kill anybody or anything."

"That was just another . . ." Kelroy began.

"There's no time for interesting facts!" screamed Zucchini.

"Ainsley, if Kelroy and I use these frongle-blasters, you can be sure they're OK. I promise. Just fire at one fishface and you'll see what I mean."

"OK, Larry, we trust you," said Ainsley, and she meant it. They had been through a lot together already, and now they were going into battle. It wasn't the time to doubt her partners.

The Chocolion led the way down to the beach. He was joined by the four cats, Choo Choo, Co Co, Rico, and Scramble, in cat armor, and Log staggering under the weight of his hammer, and then Zucchini, Zanzibar, and Bikini leading the Bow army.

Zanzibar looked at Zucchini. "Power up!"

Out of their pockets, the Bows each produced a large golden ring, and slid them onto the middle finger of their right hand. Pressing a small button on the underside of their rings the tops started to glow a brilliant white. It was as though the Bows had torches shining from their fists.

"Do I want to know what those are for?" Ainsley asked.

"I know I do." Harlan was curious as ever.

"These are sleepy-bye rings," Zucchini said. "Get touched by one even gently and it's nighty-night! We Bows have been using zem for years."

Ainsley squinted at Zanzibar's hand. "Are you sure you didn't just pick them up for a quarter or at one of those supermarket machines?"

"You'll be asleep pretty quickly if you're not careful," grumbled Zanzibar.

"C'mon, let's go," said Zootfrog to the massive frongle battalion. Larry and Kelroy stood motionless alongside Water Bucket Head, Vacuum Cleaner Brain, Quack Quack Bric-a-Brac, and Jingle Bells Batman Smells.

"I'm not sure how useful a tiny horse will be," Zucchini said.

"Trust me, he packs a punch," said Larry.

"That's just another interesting fact about Martian horses," added Kelroy.

Zucchini rolled his eyes. Meanwhile, Macklin stood ready in his white armor, while Lightning Rod hovered overhead, a look of grim determination on his face. Finally, there stood Harlan and Ainsley Banana, armed to the teeth with frongle-blasters, and scared beyond belief, although they probably shouldn't have been as worried as they were. They were surrounded by heroic companions, and, anyway, does this seem like the kind of book that's going to let them get killed in a war? I think we know each other better than that by now.

Still, they didn't know what kind of story they were in, as they watched the water bubble and boil. It was pretty scary. Dolphins, sharks, and strange pale humanoids were throwing themselves in all directions just below the surface. Every now and then, they caught a glimpse of Georgina, locked in battle with pale fishface soldiers.

Suddenly, there was a small explosion and more than two dozen fishface soldiers broke the surface, yards from shore, heading straight for land.

Larry and Kelroy sounded their novelty Lord of Bark trumpets in a loud fanfare. William's theme music picked up the tune and blared inspiring music over the unusual army assembled on the beach. It dipped in volume perfectly in time for Zootfrog, dazzling in her golden frongle armor, to yell, "For frongles, Bows, Chocolions, Martians, cats, and all other land-going creatures. For our brothers and sisters, the dolphins and the sharks. For Harlan and Ainsley. For the people of Fruitfly Bay. Let's kick some fishface butt!"

William led the way. Soaring high above their heads, he gave his music time to strike a dramatic chord, and then plunged into the midst of the fishface soldiers, who panicked and scattered from the force of his fearless attack. Harlan and Ainsley had a moment to take in the fishface for the first time. They looked vaguely human, with ghost-white skin and webbed feet and hands. They could swim fast, but they could also walk and use their hands like humans.

The fishface had huge shoulders, the result of thousands of years of swimming, and giant eyes, as you would expect of a race that lived deep underwater, so far from the sun. They wore pale armor the color of their skin, and carried seaweed whips, fishbone swords, and guns full of shark-teeth bullets. The cats huddled together as a spray of shark teeth plowed into the beach near their paws, but then Lightning Rod arrived like a tumbling comet of pure light. The fishface screamed in fright.

Zootfrog gave a strange frongle cry and charged. Her army followed, and Ainsley watched the frongles buzz and zoom through the sky, letting fly with their blasters, which emitted purple bolts of light. Fishface warriors disappeared as the light hit them.

Ainsley yelled, "The frongle-blasters are vaporizing them! You said they didn't kill!"

"No," said Larry. "Not vaporized. Fish-orized."

But there was no more time for talk. The first group of fishface soldiers had only been an advance party. Suddenly, hundreds, no, thousands of fishface troops emerged from the surf. Harlan's knees trembled and Ainsley clenched her teeth as row after row of pale, large-eyed creatures broke the surface. There were barely two hundred defenders of the land, including

Bows, frongles, cats, Martians, humans, Martian pets, and one large lion.

As the fishface advanced through the surf, the Chocolion stood completely still, barely breathing, not a muscle moving. The moment the front line of fishface soldiers cleared the water, everything changed. A growl split the air, so loud and so ferocious that several hundred fishface dived back into the sea, straight into the waiting fins of the dolphins and sharks fighting a rearguard action in the deep.

The remaining fishface soldiers had nowhere to turn. Even though they'd yearned to live on dry land, the fishface had spent thousands of years living in the water. On dry land, they had trouble walking, let alone defending themselves against an enraged Chocolion in all his glory. The lion carved massive holes in their ranks, slashing and growling and biting any pale creatures in his way. But even he could take out only a thousand or so. There were more arriving on land to the left and the right of his assault. Macklin toggled a lever on his remote control, playing with time so that he could freeze the fishface army in front of him just long enough to lay waste to five hundred of them with his frongle-blaster. Where the fishface soldiers had stood, there were now tiny fish, gently flopping about.

"Minnows!" Harlan exclaimed. "Dad uses them when we go fishing. Where did all the minnows come from?"

"Those aren't minnows. That's fishface," Larry said. "See, frongle-blasters don't kill them, they just turn them into little bitty harmless fishies."

Macklin laughed. "Those fishface are a waste of space."

Ainsley had seen enough. She gripped her frongle-blaster and decided to make some fish. She joined Harlan, Larry, Kelroy, and the four cats as they charged at another battalion of fishface struggling onto the sand.

"Why wait to make bait?" said Harlan, letting fly with his frongle-blaster. It jumped and spat in his hand as purple bolts turned fishface after fishface into small, flipping fish. Strangely, the frongle-blaster became cool in his hand as he used it. Alongside him, Ainsley was turning fishface into fish faster than cotton candy disappearing at a school carnival.

Harlan lost track of how many fishface were emerging from the waves. He was blasting and blasting purple bolts. All of a sudden, he heard a sound behind him and felt a stab of fear as he swung around, knowing he didn't have time to fire if the fishface soldiers were swarming toward him. But then Ainsley took aim with her frongle-blaster and a blur of purple produced a pile of minnows at his feet. "Thanks, Sis," said Harlan.

The battle raged along the length of the beach, with Martian pets chasing terrified fishface soldiers back into the water here, the Chocolion growling and wrestling fishface soldiers there. Co Co, Choo Choo, Scramble, and Rico let loose volley after volley of purple bolts, occasionally stopping for a fine snack of fresh minnows.

Ainsley could barely see through the smoke of the frongle-blasters. Walking toward the water, she tripped on the remains of a sand castle and sprawled onto the sand. In a second, three fishface soldiers were on top of her, whips swinging and swords ready to strike. She covered her face and screamed, expecting the worst, but instead she felt a strange fluttering against her cheek. When she opened her eyes, there were three small fish flopping on the sand. Harlan stood by her, his frongle-blaster humming. "Thanks, Bro," Ainsley said.

Harlan swung a glance back up the beach only to see Zucchini, Zanzibar, Bikini, and the other Bows still in their original position. The Bows had not joined the battle.

"What are you doing, Zucchini? Why aren't you fighting?"

"We're waiting."

"Waiting?" Harlan shouted. "Waiting for what?"

"Zee quest."

"The quest?" repeated Harlan.

"*Our* quest?" asked Ainsley.

Zucchini fixed them with a look that was surprisingly serious for a Bow. "I signed on to help you complete a Kazillion Wish quest, and a noble one at zat. I'm not about to let a small matter of a fishie-face war get in zee way of my mission. My fellow Bows have come to assist me."

"But what do you mean?" Ainsley yelled. "How can you think about the quest at a time like this? And, anyway, we're so far behind. We haven't even got our word from the Lord of Bark."

Zucchini looked at them with a gleam in his eye. "Zat is about to change, my little Banana friends. You see, zee fishie-faces would not be able to plan a land attack on their own. They need help from above zee waves, and I think our valiant partners are getting close to zee very heart of their ranks. Let's see who's been helping them out, shall we?"

Harlan and Ainsley turned back to the waves. Fish-face soldiers were still surfacing to replace the growing piles of tiny minnows flippering around in the shallows, but there was no doubt about it, the fishface ranks were thinning. As the battle continued, occasional groups of fierce fishface emerged from the deep, but many looked as though they had lost their appetite for the fight.

The Chocolion was buried so deep in minnows that he could barely be seen, while Zootfrog and the frongles were holding their own. Macklin, Larry, and Kelroy, along with the Martian pets, had all but secured the northern end of the beach, and William was so confident of victory, he was zooming up and down the shoreline, high above the action, allowing his theme music to work its way up to a triumphant victory song.

Down near a rock pool, fishface soldiers were launching into the air, giant arms flailing as they turned somersaults, then crashed into the sand unconscious.

"What's going on?" Ainsley asked.

"Look carefully," said Larry. "We're very proud of our little horse."

Sure enough, the tiny stallion Jingle Bells Batman Smells was in the thick of the action, kicking and tossing enemy soldiers into the air.

"Never get a Martian horse angry," said Kelroy.

"They're small but they're feisty," said Larry. "And so is your little friend. Look."

"I don't believe it!" said Harlan.

"It couldn't be!" said Ainsley.

But it was. Log the guinea pig was right alongside the little Martian horse, flailing at the fishface warriors with his hammer and a load of guinea pig fury. "Yahoo! Here's one for the rodents!" they heard him squeal above the fray.

Still, the sixty-strong Bow army hadn't moved, despite the chaos around them. They were focused on the point where the largest waves were breaking. Harlan squinted in that direction. And then he saw it. A small, white dog with brown spots and a fishbowl scuba mask over his head hurtled out of the surf on a flame-powered skateboard, accompanied by two adult skateboarding humans.

Georgina surfaced right behind them, but she could only wave her arms, grabbing air, as the trio shot out of her reach and into the sky toward the beach.

"It's the Lord of Bark!" screamed Harlan.

"And those good-for-nothings, Grassmuncher and Stranglenose!" shrieked Zucchini. "C'mon, Bows . . . for the sake of zee quest!"

"The quest!" screeched Zucchini's companions.

Sixty Bows shot into the sky, splitting into three

groups as they chased the Lord of Bark, Ms. Grassmuncher's evil souvenir-selling sister, and Mr. Stranglenose's nasty souvenir-selling brother around the bay.

The trio didn't have a chance. Within seconds, the Bows had surrounded them and were delivering particularly hard Bow greetings, over and over again. A couple of Bows swung their sleepy-bye rings toward Grassmuncher and Stranglenose, and they immediately slumped to the sand, snoring. Battered and sore, the Lord of Bark was led back to the beach, where the final fishface resistance was being mopped up by the frongles.

Zucchini looked pleased with himself as he escorted a sodden, beaten Lord of Bark back to his companions.

"Moments ago he was an arch-villain aiming to take over Fruitfly Bay, if not zee world. Now, thanks to us Bows, he's just a little dripping-wet dog," Zucchini announced.

"Bite me," said the Lord of Bark, but his voice carried the sound of defeat.

"Watch it, dog. We could send you back into the water and let the sharks do just that," growled the Chocolion.

The Lord of Bark quaked at the sheer size and presence of the Chocolion. "No, I surrender. I give up. You win. I'll come quietly," the small dog squeaked.

"Not so fast, Mr. Bark." Harlan made his way to the front of the group. "I asked you once before for a word and you swooped me with your skateboard."

The Lord of Bark regained a little of his toughness.

"Oh, I remember — at the tree. Stupid kid. I thought you were going to cry when I flew away. You human kids aren't so tough."

"I've asked politely once and I'll demand — *politely* — once more. Can we please have the word we need for our Kazillion Wish quest?"

"Go sleep with fleas," said the dog.

Ainsley had a definite look in her eye as she gripped her frongle-blaster. "Zootfrog? I've seen what these blasters do to fishface. What effect do they have on small dogs?"

The Lord of Bark turned a little pale. "Hey, hang on a second!"

Zootfrog was smiling as she hovered next to Ainsley's shoulder. "I don't really know, Ainsley. It might be an interesting experiment."

"He might turn into doggie poo-poo!" Zucchini was bouncing up and down.

"Or a dog biscuit." Zanzibar was bouncing, too.

"Or a small car!" Bikini shrieked.

Everybody looked at her.

"OK, probably not a small car." She shrugged.

Ainsley leaned in close to the Lord of Bark and said very deliberately, "He might even turn into a cat."

"He should be so lucky," said Choo Choo.

But Ainsley's words had found their mark. The Lord of Bark sagged and was nothing but a little frightened pooch.

"OK. Not a cat. I can't risk being a cat," he whimpered. "I give up. Have my word."

He turned to Harlan and said simply, "Are."

Zucchini bounced up and down in fury. "Ar? Ar what? Ar ar? Like a pirate? You crazy dog!"

"No, 'are,' you dumb Bow," snapped the dog. "A-R-E. Are. That is my word."

Zucchini bounced even harder. "Are, far, car, star, jar, bar, tar, Zanzibar — eh, zat's you, Cousin! — stellar, na-na-na-na, Rockefeller, Rhumbarella, Cinderella, wongazellar!"

"Wongazellar?" asked Harlan.

"A Bow ice-cream flavor. Delicious," said Zucchini.

Ainsley frowned. "'Here's the thing birds are . . .' I still don't get what this all means."

Georgina had joined them on the beach. "You are so, so, so, so close."

Zootfrog hovered nearby. "Georgina is right. It doesn't make sense because you're still two words away from completion, but you are very close. Remember, the next word must come from our friends who cut the foam. I think the dolphins will prove much easier to persuade than nasty, cruel little dogs with ideas of world domination."

"Hey!" said the Lord of Bark.

"Georgina, I need to ask you something," said Harlan suddenly. "It's about your mother."

"My mother? OK. But first, I'm going to help you get your dolphin word!"

Ainsley was already donning her frongle scuba goggles and wading into the surf. Harlan shrugged.

Georgina was right; it could wait. They were so close to the end of the quest. He dived under the waves.

Underwater, dolphins and sharks were nursing wounded comrades, with medical teams led by octopus doctors and starfish assistants moving from injured group to injured group. All around, piled from the sand far below to near the surface, were giant mountains of minnows. The dolphins and sharks had clearly taken the brunt of the fishface attack before the enemy even made it anywhere near dry land.

"Over there!" shouted Ainsley. The dolphin king and the giant whale shark leader were swimming gracefully through the battle zone, checking on their troops. King Dorsal spotted the children and swam over, nodding wisely.

"Congratulations to you all in this moment of victory. Georgina, you have done us proud today. I intend to award you with our highest dolphin honor: the Order of Flipper."

"Thank you, King Dorsal," said Georgina.

The dolphin king turned to Harlan and Ainsley. "As for you, Banana children, my scouts report that you fought valiantly. Truly, you are special children, and I thank you on behalf of all dolphins."

"And I on behalf of all sharks," said the whale shark in a booming deep voice.

"Even the Great Whites?" said Harlan, unable to help himself.

Georgina smiled. "I used to be scared of them, too."

"They're just misunderstood," said the whale shark. "You get a couple of bad apples and it spoils it for everybody."

"I'll have to take your word for it," said Ainsley. "King Dorsal, Your Highness, could we trouble you for one more thing? I know you're busy with your wounded dolphins, but we are very close to the end of our Kazillion Wish quest, and Zootfrog suggested we ask you for our word."

"Ah yes, the quest continues." The dolphin king smiled. "I don't mind at all, Ainsley. In fact, the wake of such a glorious triumph seems like the perfect time to honor a noble quest. The word you require is 'not.'"

"Is not what?" Zucchini shrieked, having swum up beside them, giant notebook at the ready — and apparently waterproof. "Zee word is not ready? Is not suitable? Is not available? Is not to be uttered? Is not for human consumption? Is not for zis world?"

"Relax, Bow." King Dorsal laughed. "Yet again, you have misheard. You should learn to listen. Our word is 'not,' and 'not' is our word. N-O-T, not."

Ainsley put it all together. "Here's the thing birds are not."

Harlan frowned. "Birds are not land-dwellers? Birds are not large? Birds are not furry?"

Georgina and the dolphin king chuckled. "One word to go and the quest is yours," said King Dorsal.

"All you have to do is close your eyes," Georgina said.

Harlan and Ainsley looked at each other.

"The final task in the poem," Harlan said.

> *"'You must help our friends*
> *Who cut the foam,*
> *And talk to those*
> *Who dreamward roam.'"*

King Dorsal spoke up:

> *"'Then a Kazillion Wish*
> *Shall be yours*
> *As long as noble*
> *Be your cause.'"*

"Good luck, Bananas."

"Thank you," said Ainsley. "Thank you so much, dolphins and sharks. Come on, Harlan, we'd better get back to Fruitfly Bay."

A dolphin who'd been hovering nearby said, "Can I offer you a lift?"

"Yes, please," chorused the children.

13

Nighty-Night, Bananas

Back on the beach, everybody was tucking into a fish lunch, although Log the guinea pig was munching contentedly on grass from the shore.

"Big day," said Larry.

"I'm certainly ready for lunch," Kelroy agreed.

"Today will go down in Bow history as one of our greatest victories!" Zucchini declared.

"What? The Bows hardly even fought," the Chocolion protested. "You just stood around, waiting for that little dog to appear. I saw only two Bows touch a couple of fishface soldiers with cheap supermarket novelty rings!"

"Sometimes zee greatest warriors are great because they await their moment," said Zucchini.

"Await their destiny," agreed Bikini.

"Await their ultimate foe," added Zanzibar.

"Await their knees to stop shaking," mumbled Macklin.

"Await clean underwear," said William.

"Await everybody else to do the work," growled the Chocolion.

"Ah well, whatever. . . . Who's gonna write zee Bow victory songs? You or us? Suckers!" Zucchini said.

"There's just one thing, Zucchini," Ainsley said, sitting on the sand. "We've got one word to go and we have to talk to those who dreamward roam."

"Sounds easy." Zucchini shrugged. "Nighty-night."

The Bananas stared at him. "But it's the middle of the day."

"And we're not the least bit tired," said Harlan. "In fact, my heart is still pounding from the battle. I couldn't possibly go to sleep."

"I could hit you with my hammer," squeaked the guinea pig.

"Thanks, Log. We appreciate the offer, but no," Ainsley said. "We don't even know how to find the ones who dreamward roam, even if we did go to sleep."

Bikini laughed. "How hard can it be? Lots of snores, a few dreams. There you are and there zey are."

"There who are? I mean is? I mean . . . oh, you know what I mean," Harlan said.

Zootfrog spoke up. "The dreamers. Otherwise known as Princess Bella and Princess Ruby."

"The Princesses of zee Slumberworld," said Zucchini, loving the confusion written all over the faces. "It's time you went to say hello."

"Huh?" said Harlan and Ainsley, together.

"Nighty-night." With a flick of his finger and a zooming sound, Zucchini's sleepy-bye ring suddenly shone with white light, and with it he touched first Harlan, then Ainsley. The pair slumped to the ground, sound asleep.

Moments later, Harlan was in a green field, with soft grass under his bare feet and tree branches waving gently around him. The sun was warm on his back. He felt content, as though he'd just enjoyed a large plate of chocolate cake with ice cream. Birds sang in the trees and small animals gently nuzzled him, in search of a cuddle or a pat.

Harlan became aware of his sister, standing beside him.

"Where are we? What happened?" she asked. "We're not at Fruitfly Bay. Where are the others?"

"I think we're about to find out. Someone's coming." Harlan was gazing across the field.

A girl, about ten years old, was walking toward them. She had bare feet, and colorful ankle bracelets, and she wore a flowing, white dress decorated with pearls and jewels that glinted in the sun. The girl had beautiful brown hair, entwined with ribbons and bows and jewelry. Around her neck was a magnificent chain, intensely green, and on her wrists were bracelets of spectacular diamonds, sapphires, and emeralds.

"Cool outfit!" said Ainsley.

"Are you an angel?" whispered Harlan.

The girl smiled. "Hello, Harlan and Ainsley. I'm Princess Bella."

"We're asleep, aren't we?" Ainsley said.

Harlan nodded. "You're one of the ones who dreamward roam."

"That is correct, Harlan. Welcome to your dreams."

"Wow!" Ainsley put her hands to her mouth. "You can give us our final word!"

"To complete our noble quest," said Harlan. "Oh, please, tell us the word, Princess!"

"Well, I would, but I don't think you're really asleep."

"What are you talking about? Of course I'm asleep," said Harlan.

"Perhaps you are, but you're about to wake up."

"No, I'm not. Why would you say that?"

"Because there's a Bow about to stick a feather up your nose."

"HEY!"

Back on the Fruitfly Bay beach, Harlan sat up suddenly and belted Zucchini's hand away from his nose. "I'm trying to sleep here."

"Sorry. Just a little Bow joke," said Zucchini. "Nighty-night again."

He prodded him with his sleepy-bye ring and Harlan crumpled again.

"Where were we?" asked Princess Bella.

"That crazy Bow," grumbled Harlan. "We were asking for our word."

"Oh yes, of course. But wouldn't you like to look around first?"

Harlan and Ainsley looked at each other. "Well, maybe briefly," said Ainsley, who didn't want to be rude.

Princess Bella smiled. "I know how badly you want your word, but relax, you're almost there. Come see our world. Cloud or car?"

That wasn't a choice the Bananas had been offered before.

"Car, please," said Harlan.

Immediately, a cherry red car appeared. It had no roof and was just the right size for kids. Bella got in the front and the Bananas sat in the back. Princess Bella drove off fast, dodging trees and animals.

"I can't believe you didn't ask for a cloud," Ainsley hissed. "She offered to take us on a cloud! Did you hear her? A cloud! And you said *car*!"

Princess Bella was talking to them over her shoulder as she drove. "This is Happy Valley. This is a great place to come in your dreams if you just feel like relaxing in your sleep."

Harlan had to think about that. "Isn't that all you ever do in your sleep?"

"Oh no," said Princess Bella. "We're just coming to Action Land, which is where all the dramatic, exciting dreams take place. You know, when you dream about being a superhero? Or flying in space? Or winning a big football match? Or being a pop star? All of those dreams happen in Action Land. Ainsley, I've seen you here many times."

Ainsley grinned. "How many people can you fit in the Slumberworld at once?" she asked.

"Everybody on Earth. Your dreams are limitless."

Action Land was behind them now and the landscape

had become very strange, with trees made of ice, waterfalls running with jelly, and penguins with megaphones instead of beaks.

Ainsley waved to one of the penguins, who boomed back, "HOWDY!"

Ainsley got such a shock she almost fell out of the car.

"This is Fantasy Land, where all the really weird dreams take place," Bella explained. "Harlan, you've spent a lot of nights here, although you probably don't remember it in the morning. Your imagination is fantastic."

"What sort of dreams do you have here?" asked Ainsley.

"This is where you come if you happen to dream about having nine legs and flying like a bat, or of swimming through space, or of dancing on a pinhead . . . or of being a ghostlike puff of steam."

"A ghostlike puff of steam? Who would dream of being a ghostlike puff of steam?" Harlan frowned.

"I don't know . . . steam, maybe. Coming up on the right, Comedy Land. This is where funny dreams take place."

As they cruised past, they saw a boy dressed in his pajamas, walking along the street. Suddenly, he slipped on a banana peel, completely lost his balance, crashed headfirst into a lemon meringue pie at a bakery stall, staggered blindly along the sidewalk, tripped again, and splashed face-first into a puddle of water. He reeled backward and sat heavily on a whoopee cushion. *Bllaaaarrrtt.*

Bella and the Banana kids almost wet themselves laughing.

"Slumberworld is incredible!" Harlan said. "Do you actually live here, Bella?"

"We live in a dream castle, on the hill," she said, pointing. "We keep an eye on all these worlds to make sure nobody is having a bad dream. Everybody here is supposed to have a good time while they're asleep. The bad dreams happen farther down the road."

"You said where *we* live. Who else lives there?"

"My sister. You're about to meet her. Look out!"

The car was suddenly shrouded in darkness. The sky had been getting gloomy but now it was as though a giant shadow had fallen over the car.

Harlan saw a cloud hovering directly above their heads, keeping pace with them.

Suddenly, a girl's face appeared over one edge of the cloud. "BOO!"

Bella swerved to keep control. "Ruby!" she yelled. "I hate it when you do that!"

The cloud took off. It roared away in front of them, spun in the air, and then flew back at them. Ruby was smiling wickedly as she closed in on the car.

"Very pleased to meet you, Bananas!" she said, skimming over their heads and dropping a handful of large, fat spiders into their laps. Ainsley yelped and started pitching spiders over the side while Harlan sat frozen in his seat, unable to move. He *hated* spiders.

"Ruby!" shouted Bella, stopping the car. "Please excuse my sister. She's in charge of Yikesville, and sometimes she gets a little carried away. She doesn't mean any harm. She's just teasing you."

"Yikesville?" Harlan managed to ask as Ainsley sent the last spider over the side of the car. Ainsley saw it high-five one of the other spiders, using five legs. In a tiny little spider voice, it said, "Oh yeah!"

"Yikesville is where the nightmares happen. Lots of ghosts, spiders, slugs, monsters, and other things that make their living playing bad guys in nightmares. Horrible place."

"Slugs can make a living out of being bad guys?" Ainsley said.

"Why is it called Yikesville?" asked Harlan.

"Because so many people realize they're having a nasty nightmare and wake up, yelling, 'Yikes!'"

Ruby hovered closer. "You should have seen your faces! Zucchini Spacestation would have been proud of me."

"You know Zucchini?"

"Sure, he has a lot of nightmares . . . full of images of butterflies."

"Butterflies? Butterflies aren't scary."

"Hey, don't ask me how a Bow brain works." Ruby shrugged.

"You're assuming they have a brain," added Bella.

"You do know Zucchini," said Harlan. "Is there any chance we can move on from Yikesville?"

"I kind of like it here," said Ainsley, watching two gleaming eyes stare out from under a rock.

"We were going to make you spend a whole night here, to earn your quest word," Ruby said. "But after the way you fought off the fishface, we decided you'd more than earned it already."

"Thank you," said Harlan.

"Ruby, is there a chance I could have a ride on your cloud?" Ainsley asked. "And go fast!"

"Of course," she replied.

Soon they were back in Happy Valley, the sun warm on their backs and peace restored.

"So, I suppose you want your word?" Ruby said.

"Please!"

Bella laughed. "I hope the quest has been worth it. You must want an also-mom very much."

"We just want our dad to be happy again," Ainsley said.

"Yeah, no more sad songs and moping." Harlan nodded.

Princess Bella smiled. "Good luck, kids. You deserve it. Your final word is 'fish.'"

The children stared at her. Eventually, Bella said, "You don't seem very pleased."

"Are you *sure* that's the word?"

"Of course we're sure, Harlan," said Princess Ruby. "Do you think we'd give you the wrong word when you're one word away from finishing a Kazillion Wish quest?"

"And a noble one at that," added Bella. "'Fish' is definitely the right word."

"Congratulations," said Ruby. "Time to wake up."

"How do we do that?" asked Harlan. "I've never tried to wake up from within a dream before." Which was true, because Harlan was a lazy sleepyhead who liked to dream on for as long as possible before school.

Bella said, "Well, a Bow is about to stick a grasshopper up your nose. That should help."

14

Birds, Not Even a Bit Like Fish

"**H**EY!" Harlan woke suddenly, back in Fruitfly Bay. "Cut it out!"

"Just a little Bow joke," said Zucchini. "If zere's one thing we Bows love, it's playing tricks on people while they're asleep."

"Well, knock it off," warned Ainsley. "Look! Zucchini, behind you! A butterfly!"

Zucchini leaped in the air, shrieking and hiding his head in his hands. Then he looked around and realized the air was butterfly-free. "Oh, very funny, Ainsley Banana. You have been hanging out with Princess Ruby, haven't you?"

"Zootfrog, we've got our final word!"

"Well done, Ainsley!"

"But the quest phrase doesn't make sense," said Harlan.

"Here's the thing," said Ainsley. "Birds are not fish."

Zootfrog nodded. Larry and Kelroy beamed. Georgina smiled. Zanzibar and Bikini clapped. The Chocolion's green eyes shone. William and Macklin whooped. Zucchini pulled a massive book out of his endless coat pocket, entitled *Birds: Those Flappy Wonder Fish of the Sky*, by Zucchini Spacestation.

"Well, so much for my book!" he said, throwing it away.

"Congratulations," said Zootfrog. "It was the journey that mattered, more than the words themselves. You have proven yourselves most worthy of a Kazillion Wish. You are very special children, Harlan and Ainsley Banana."

Harlan and Ainsley beamed. "Thank you," said Harlan, not knowing what else to say.

"Now what happens?" asked Ainsley.

"Now what? Now what? Now what? What now? . . . What wow? Not wow? Snot cow? Hot chow? . . . What? A SNOT COW?" said Zucchini, building up to something. "What happens now is . . . *a Bow party!*"

An enormous rainbow formed near the Bows' feet. It stretched way up into the sky, and the children could faintly make out a building at the top.

"The Starry Eye Café," explained Zanzibar. "Where else would we party? The rainbow is a shortcut."

Harlan studied the base of the rainbow. "Hey, Zucchini, where is the sandbox?"

"Sandbox?" said the Bow. "What sandbox?"

"Zootfrog told us that Bows needed a sandbox to land in when you come down a rainbow slide. She said we humans thought it was gold, but it was to cushion your fall."

Zootfrog laughed quietly.

"Oh yeah, laugh it up, frongle," said Zucchini. "Very funny. Harlan, I think you should know by now zat an elite Bow such as myself hardly needs a sandbox to help him step off a rainbow. I'll pretend we never had zis conversation."

Zucchini stalked over to the rainbow, intending to lead the way up to the café. Unfortunately, he tripped over a large pile of sand and whacked his head on the side of the rainbow's colored bars. There was a loud honking sound, and when he stood up, his entire face was purple, orange, green, blue, red, and yellow.

"I hate it when I do zat!" he said, but he was smiling. "Come on, everybody. To zee party!... Harlan and Ainsley, you have to wait until last."

"Why?" asked Ainsley.

Zucchini looked sly. "It's a secret."

Harlan shook his head and laughed. It was just starting to sink in that they had actually completed their quest. Harlan impersonated Zucchini's crazy French accent as he said, "You know what, Zucchini?... Secrets *are* fun!"

15

The Party to End All Parties

It was incredible. The parking lot of the Starry Eye Café had been converted into a giant party space. Everyone was there. Harlan and Ainsley couldn't believe their eyes. They arrived at the top of the rainbow to be greeted by the biggest round of applause they had ever heard.

The waiters were frongles, hovering in the air with giant trays of drinks and food. Harlan and Ainsley grabbed ladybug milk shakes and settled into a flurry of slaps on the backs, hugs, and congratulations.

Ainsley took in the crowd. Larry was talking to William, whose Lightning Rod music was playing a dance tune with a strong beat. Bikini Spacestation was dancing with Vacuum Cleaner Brain. Macklin was busy in the café itself, turning out Starry Eye–specials —

pineapple frintoburgers, toasted strawberry ice-cream stir-fries, and chocolate-coated cronkofruit biscuits.

Co Co, Choo Choo, Rico, and Scramble sat on the dome-shaped roof, arms around one another as they sang:

"Oh, Don Gato
Was a Spanish cat...
On a high red roof,
Don Gato sat..."

"I didn't realize cats were such lousy singers," said Ainsley.

Kelroy was dancing with Zanzibar Spacestation, while an important-looking frongle was talking to the orangutan that worked in the Chocolion's waiting room. The Chocolion was talking to Georgina. Meanwhile, Zootfrog danced a frongle dance that took place more in the air than on the ground. She was accompanied by King Dorsal, who was wearing sunglasses — presumably the dolphin equivalent of frongle scuba goggles so that he could safely spend time out of the water.

Ainsley was surprised to see Princess Bella dancing along with Water Bucket Head, a couple of frongles, and Zucchini Spacestation, who was pulling off some remarkable Bow moves. Princess Ruby was floating overhead, giving Quack Quack Bric-a-Brac a warm duck cuddle from her cloud.

"I'm surprised William hasn't started dancing yet," said Harlan. "He dances every chance he gets."

"Actually, he and Macklin are busy spiking zee ladybug shakes with Lightning Juice," said Zucchini, panting from all his dancing.

Harlan noticed the Lord of Bark's evil assistants, Grassmuncher and Stranglenose, sitting dejectedly outside a small shed near the back of the café. "Zucchini, what happened to the Lord of Bark?"

Zucchini pointed to the shed. "He's in there. Little Barky Sad Pants doesn't get to join in zee party after all his evil nonsense. When we've finished celebrating, William plans to make him sit in zat giant tree for a few days to have a good hard think about his behavior. Then we're not sure. . . . He probably needs to go back to puppy school."

They all laughed, especially when Harlan pointed out Jingle Bells Batman Smells dancing with Log the guinea pig.

Feeling happier than he could remember, Harlan made his way over to the counter and took two glasses of ladybug milk shake from Macklin, who smiled innocently.

The children clinked glasses. "To us, Sis. We did it. We completed a Kazillion Wish quest."

Ainsley sipped. "I still can't believe it."

Georgina approached, also sipping a ladybug milk shake. "Hi, Bananas. You must be over the moon. As I said when we met, I only know of one other person who has earned a Kazillion Wish. It's a great achievement."

Harlan's eyes lit up. "It was you, wasn't it, Georgina? And it involved the water. That's why you're so friendly with the dolphins!"

Georgina smiled. "Close, but not quite. It wasn't me. It was my mother."

"Your mother! Wow!" said Harlan. "Hey, Larry and Kelroy said that your mother knows our father."

"She does?"

"Yes. Larry said we should ask you about it."

"What's your father's name?"

"Spencer Banana."

Georgina squinted, searching her memory. "That name *is* familiar. Let me think about it."

Ainsley sipped her ladybug milk shake. "There's something else I want to know."

"What's that?"

"How do we know if the Kazillion Wish has been granted?"

"What?" said Zucchini, gulping down his fifth glass of ladybug milk shake. "Do you mean, how will you know if your father has met somebody he likes so much zat she could become your also-mom and zey could live happily, happily, happily ever after?"

"Well . . . yeah," said Harlan. "Pretty much."

Zucchini shrugged. "Here he comes now. Why don't you ask him?"

There, edging his way through the teeming crowd

of Martians, frongles, Bows, animals, dolphins, and a giant lion, was their father. He was working his way toward them with a huge smile on his face.

"I thought it was such a good party that it was time he woke up from our spell," Zootfrog whispered, floating past.

Harlan and Ainsley threw themselves into his arms. "Dad!" they yelled.

Their father gave them both a huge, bone-splintering hug. "This is quite a party," he said. "I'm assuming these creatures are friends of yours."

Their father was pretty unflappable.

"Mostly," said Harlan. "Though I could live without the little dog in the shed over there, and the two nasty people sitting outside it."

Dad looked at Grassmuncher and Stranglenose, as they grudgingly accepted ladybug milk shakes from Lightning Rod. "They look familiar."

"It's not what you're thinking," said Harlan. "Don't you dare mention this party on parent-teacher night."

"OK, but don't expect a repeat of this for your birthday party." Spencer Banana looked around and watched Kelroy trying to form a conga chain, which is tricky when you have five legs, with Log the guinea pig, who only comes up to your five knees.

Finally, Spencer bent down so he was at Ainsley's eye level. "What have you been up to, Second Banana?"

"They can't tell you, I'm afraid," said Zootfrog, flying up to hover near their father's head. "Secret kid-and-frongle business. But trust me, they've done it all for you."

"Done what for me?"

"Like I said, it's a secret." Zootfrog smiled.

"Zootfrog, when will we get our wish?" Ainsley whispered.

"You'll just have to be patient." Zootfrog smiled. "You can't hurry love."

Just then, Zucchini bustled up to their dad.

"Mr. Banananananananananananana! Hello, hello, hello! It's verrrrry nice to meet you." Zucchini's accent seemed more outrageous than ever.

Spencer gave Harlan a quick glance that either meant his allowance had just been cut in half or he wanted Harlan to call the police. Possibly both. "And you'd be?"

"Aha! Aha! Aha! I'm very glad you asked. I'm *so* glad you asked. It's magnificent that you asked! Allow me to introduce myself." Zucchini drew himself up to his full height (not very tall) and paused dramatically. "I am me, me is I, zat is me, and who I be is me, me, me, me, me. In fact, O Great Father of zee Most Wondrous Banana Two, I'd like to tell you my name. Yes, my name! My name is . . ." He paused again, and held his pose.

"He always does this," whispered Harlan to his dad, rolling his eyes.

"My name is ZUCCHINI SPACESTATION! . . . Z is for Zoo, U is for Umbrella. C is for Cabbage. Another C is for, um, Checklist. H is for Haberdashery, I is for . . . well, you get zee idea. Oh yeah, Idea! I is for Idea! I'd love to sit and talk, Mr. Banana, and tell you about zee wonderful heroics I have performed to help your children, but unfortunately, I just unthinkingly sipped my ninth ladybug milk shake and now my foot is starting to move all by itself."

"Uh-oh," said Harlan. His knees were quivering and his shoulders had started to sway. "William!"

"Go with the music, Harley Barley," grinned Lightning Rod, dancing wildly in the middle of the dance floor.

"Dance till you drop, Mr. Bop." Macklin giggled.

Harlan smiled at Ainsley and shrugged. The two of them joined everybody on the dance floor as the Lightning Juice took hold. The music was booming and even Grassmuncher and Stranglenose found themselves dancing uncontrollably in the corner — although they weren't very happy about it.

The only person not dancing was Spencer Banana, who hadn't had a drink. He was staring, transfixed, at the other side of the café.

There stood a woman, looking at the scene before her. She had straight red hair and was wearing a T-shirt with the word KITTEN emblazoned on it. Her black jacket matched her skirt and big, black boots.

"Boy, she's dressed like a superhero," said William, somehow dancing the samba, the limbo, and the funky chicken all at the same time.

Harlan and Ainsley stared at the stranger. "Dad? Who's that?" Ainsley yelled over the music.

"It's Dinah! It's Dinah Drakedown! . . . I know her! We used to be best, best friends in college. What is she doing here? I haven't seen her for years!"

Harlan and Ainsley swung around. They looked at Zootfrog with saucer eyes.

"Well, fancy that." Zootfrog was attempting an innocent frongle face.

"Don't just stand zere, Spencey-wencey!" said Zucchini. "Go and say hello, you great big bundle of lovvvvvvvvvvvvve."

Spencer began to make his way through the crowd, but then turned.

"Spencey-wencey?"

"Just go! Go! Go! Go!" Zucchini waved his hands so fast he knocked a frongle waiter flying. *Poom!*

Spencer walked as though in a daze, not even noticing the unlikely spectacle of a green Martian dog doing the rumba with an orangutan. Harlan and Ainsley could hardly breathe as they watched their father make his way through the pack of dancers. Finally, the woman saw him and her eyes grew wide.

"Spencer?" they heard her say. "Spencer Banana?"

"Dinah Drakedown?"

"I don't believe it." She threw herself into his arms and they hugged like two people who haven't seen each other for far too long.

Eventually, Harlan and Ainsley's dad broke out of the hug, held the woman's hand, and led her through the dancers to where they stood, unable to move, Lightning Juice or not. It was as though they were frozen. Harlan whispered, "Remember, Ainsley, you don't have to worry . . . Mom is always Mom. That never changes."

His sister whispered right back. "Also-mom."

Their dad looked happier than they could remember seeing him for a long, long time. Weaving through the dancers, the woman was saying, ". . . I just had this uncontrollable urge to come back to Fruitfly Bay . . . and now I've bumped straight into you. I can't believe it."

"But what are you doing here, at this party?"

"The same thing you are," Dinah said.

And then Georgina was next to them. "Hi, Mom."

Dinah put an arm around her. "Spencer, meet my daughter, Georgina."

Harlan broke into a huge smile. "It's your mother! The one who completed a Kazillion Wish quest!"

"A what?" said their father.

"I'll tell you all about it," said Dinah. "I'm the only human ever to have done it."

"Not anymore, Mom," Georgina said. "Meet Harlan and Ainsley Banana."

Dinah looked down at the children. "Harlan and Ainsley *Banana*. You mean?"

"Yes, these are my kids, Dinah. We've got a lot to catch up on."

"We sure do. Harlan and Ainsley, you completed a Kazillion Wish quest?"

Harlan nodded.

"And did you get your wish?"

For a moment, Ainsley couldn't answer. She just

took two quick steps forward and wrapped her arms around Dinah, giving her a hug to end all hugs.

"I think that's a yes," said Harlan.

Spencer and Dinah smiled at each other. "I've still got some of your old records," Spencer said.

"You have? Which ones?"

"Some blues. Mostly sad stuff."

"You won't be needing them anymore, Dad," said Harlan.

"You might be right, Snarlin' Harlan."

Zucchini suddenly appeared and handed Dinah a large glass.

"Here, have some ladybug milk shake."

Dinah took a sip, then put one arm around Spencer and one arm around Ainsley, who was still hugging her fiercely. "Tell me, Spencer Banana, have you missed me?"

Spencer looked suddenly serious. "Like my body would miss its heart."

"Good line," Bikini said to Zucchini. "We'll have to remember zat."

Georgina was standing next to Harlan. "Are you sure about this, Harlan? Are you sure this is the wish you want?"

"It is, if it's OK with you."

"The look on Mom's face is all I need to see."

Harlan smiled and nodded, then joined his sister in hugging Dinah, who winked at Zucchini and Zootfrog.

"You know what? I have a feeling that Harlan, Ainsley, and I are going to get along just fine."

"Forever," mumbled Ainsley from somewhere near Dinah's stomach.

"What was that?" asked Spencer Banana.

Harlan beamed at Georgina, Zootfrog, and Zucchini. "She said, 'happily ever after.'"

Acknowledgments

An enormous thank-you to Barry the Boss Chook and all the rest of the Chickens for so much enthusiasm, energy, and creativity in bringing *The Kazillion Wish* to the world. Thanks also to Ross Collins for his spectacular drawings. And thanks to everyone at Allen & Unwin, the Australian publishers — especially editor Jodie and publisher Rosalind for picking up an unsolicited manuscript, laughing out loud, and thinking that was enough to go on.